WHO AM I?

Using the Book

This book can be read like a normal book. However, to make it more interesting, we have included a flap at the end. Use this flap to make a game out of the book.

Each page has four chunks of information on one person. Use the flap to show one info block at a time, and try to identify the gender of the person first and then the special characteristics of the person or the field in which he or she acquired eminence. The fourth clue more or less tells you the person. Below the info blocks, you can see a picture connected to the personality and you get to know something more about him or her.

Fold the sheet to show clues as shown in the figures.

Fold once to show the first clue. Able to guess the person and answer it correct? If so, you must have read the *Who's Who* or the *Encyclopaedia Britannica*?

Fold again to show the second clue. Correct answer? Get some 15 points. Your brain deserves to be kept in a museum.

Fold to the third clue. A correct answer at this stage gets you 10. You may not have read the *Who's Who* or the *Encyclopaedia* but you do have some general knowledge.

No answers yet? Fold again to see the fourth clue. This one was plain unlucky for you. Take 5 if you answer it here.

No answers? Guess what? You are actually the luckiest! You don't get any point, but you get to see the picture of the person and read some interesting tidbits about him or her.

Talk to Us

We invite readers to compile pieces of information in the style followed in this book. Try to keep some information that is interesting and seldom heard of, apart from the usual necessary information. Do not forget to include your source for the information. Send this to us with your name and address, and we will include it in an upcoming edition of the book with your name as a contributor.
So what are you waiting for? Get up and get cracking.

WHO AM I?

100 Historic Personalities of the World

Madhu Goyle
St. Columba's School, New Delhi

This book is a compilation of facts and information from various sources. However, the figures and numbers given in this work are subject to change according to time. Care has been taken to verify the contents very thoroughly up to the time of publication. In case anyone has any query, clarification, complaint or suggestion, please let us know, and we will immediately look into it. Also, in case anyone feels a credit is due, immediately write to us, and we will get back to you. Any infringement of copyright or trademark is not intended.

ISBN: 978-81-86685-79-2

First published 2005
Reprinted 2008, 2009, 2010, 2011, 2012, 2013, 2015

Published by
Wisdom Tree
4779/23, Ansari Road
Darya Ganj, New Delhi-110 002
Ph.: 011-23247966/67/68
wisdomtreebooks@gmail.com

Printed in India

Introduction

Every stream begins with a drop. Learning too begins from the first word uttered. Beginning in a small way, a learner gradually moves forward to learn more and more. In India we had the guru-*shishya parampara* where one or two students learnt from a guru or teacher by living in the same environment and under the same conditions. Gradually and slowly this gave way to formal education with learning imparted in schools. Then came the realisation that children be allowed the freedom to express themselves freely, with as little interference as possible. This approach suggested what people like Franz Cizek and many educationists were advocating — create an atmosphere in school as also in the family in which the child expresses his or her feelings, experiences and dreams with freedom and without inhibitions for full development of the child's personality — but this too proved wrong. Today the argument is that the child must be taught the right things from his/her very early years.

The aim of our book is not to impart bookish knowledge as we feel enough of that is given in schools. We found that very limited reading material is available by way of which a child could enjoy learning while reading. So under our fun-filled informative series, we decided to bring out this book along with others, which can make learning a fun-filled activity.

This book gives in brief all the landmarks in the lives of well-known personalities who have left an indelible mark in some field or the other, be it in science or humanities. Here you can read about Helen of Troy whose beauty launched a thousand ships to set sail for Troy, Queen Cleopatra of Egypt who acquired fame for her beauty than her intelligence, the great warrior-kings like Ashoka, Alexander and Akbar, scientists like Einstein, Archimedes and Newton, musicians like Mozart and Bach, painters like Leonardo da Vinci and M.F. Hussain, litterateurs like Mark Twain and Premchand — you name them and we have them. Not only will the short life-sketches enlighten you as the reader, they will arouse further curiosity and tempt you to find out more on what exactly made these personalities great.

Madhu Goyle

I am the daughter of the king of gods, Zeus, who visited my mother Leda, the queen of **Sparta**, in the form of a swan. It is also said that I am the daughter of Zeus and Nemesis, the goddess of fate, who did not want a child, and so left me in the form of a swan's egg. Leda saw the egg, and raised me when I was born. As a young child of about 13, I was kidnapped by the Athenian hero, Theseus, king of Athens, and was later rescued by my brothers.

When I grew up, word about my beauty spread far and wide and attracted a number of nobles but **antagonistic suitors**. Each of them sent me gifts and proposals through their representatives. Ulysses (or Odysseus) was also one of the suitors, and he asked everyone to support his choice. My father chose Menelaus, the brother of Agamemnon. Some of the suitors did not appear in person but sent representatives with offers of handsome dowries. I married Menelaus.

Sparta went through a plague during the early years of my marriage, and Menelaus was advised, as a part of a ritual to please the gods, to visit Troy. My husband came back with the Trojan prince, Paris. We fell in love and ran away on Paris' ship to Troy. Paris refused to surrender me. My former suitors banded together and won a 10-year long war, after which I was reunited with Menelaus. After Menelaus' death, I was exiled to Rhodes, where I was either hanged or murdered.

The war in Troy, called the Trojan War, took place in about 1184 BC. The war is famous for the wooden horse used by my suitors to rescue me. I am said to have had a 'face that launched a thousand ships'. The thousand ships refer to the troops that sailed to Troy to rescue me. **Achilles** was the leading hero of the Greeks in the Trojan War. Homer focuses on Achilles' role in the war, in *The Iliad*.

Helen of Troy

Homer's *Iliad* made Helen known to the world. Though it is said that there is plenty of fiction mixed with facts, Helen nevertheless continues to be regarded as one of the most beautiful, and written of, women that lived on earth. It is said that Homer was a blind **bard** who composed and recited *The Iliad* and *The Odyssey* a few hundred years after the events happened.

I am often portrayed as a ruthless queen. I was born in 69 BC in Alexandria, Egypt, as the daughter of the **Pharaoh** of Egypt, Ptolemy Auletes. I had two older sisters, Cleopatra VI and Berenice IV and a younger sister, Arsinoe IV. I also had two younger brothers, Ptolemy XIII and Ptolemy XIV. When my father died, I ascended the Egyptian throne. I was only 17. My sisters had already died and I was the eldest child.

According to Egyptian law, I had to have a male consort, no matter what age, throughout my reign. I was thus married to my younger brother Ptolemy XIII when he was 12. I soon dropped his name from official documents and had my own portrait and name on coins of that time. According to my face on the coins, I was far from beautiful despite what people think today. I presented myself to the Roman Emperor, wrapped in a beautiful carpet, and wonder of wonders, he fell in love with me.

Caesar fought against my brother and killed him. I again became queen with my youngest brother Ptolemy XI, who was 11-years old, as consort. I was invited to Rome by Caesar, who showered me with gifts. A gold statue of mine was placed in the temple of **Venus Genetrix**. His fellow Romans were scandalised and scared that our son might be made the heir. On 15 March 44 BC, he was stabbed to death. As I and my son were in danger, I fled to Egypt and made Caesarion the co-ruler.

I now enthralled Mark Antony. This outraged the Romans, especially Antony's co-ruler Octavian. Octavian declared war against us, and after a miserable defeat at Actium, we fled to Alexandria. Antony was defeated again, and depressed, he committed suicide. Octavian took me prisoner but I killed myself before meeting any humiliation. According to legend, I died of the bite of an **asp**, smuggled to me in a basket of figs.

Cleopatra (VII)

She, though less known for her intelligence, was an extremely intelligent woman. Cleopatra was a quick-witted woman who was fluent in nine languages. She was a mathematician and a very good businesswoman. She fought for her country. Among the legends that surround her is one that says she bathed in milk, and ate pearls dissolved in wine.

I am the son of Philip II of Macedonia, and Olympias, the daughter of Neptolemus of Epirus. My father was a great leader and brought all of Greece under his rule just before his assassination in 336 BC. I grew up in Athens, not only in the shadow of my father but of the great philosopher Aristotle, who was my teacher. He inspired in me my lifelong interest in biology, medicine and zoology. I was raised to believe that I had descended from both the Greek heroes Achilles and Herakles.

I was a brilliant and charismatic leader. Unlike most other victorious leaders, I was not only receptive to the ideas of conquered peoples but also adopted their ideas. It was my achievements as a commander on the field of battle that justify my name. I was a military genius, and a hero to my men. I personally spearheaded my attacks, suffering severe arrow, lance, sword and knife wounds. I also shared my vast riches with my men.

I had acquired a zealous reverence for the ancient Greek myths. I built an empire greater than any that had existed. It stretched from Greece to India. When I was 33, I had 50 times as much land and ruled over 20 times as many people as I had inherited from my father, Philip. My territory included all of the former Persian Empire. I even sought to find the source of **River Nile** by sending expeditions deep into Africa.

Before I made my second attempt to cross into India in 327 BC, I trained the army that accompanied me from Persia to adapt to the climate and terrain. I was so serious about this invasion that I burned my Persian booty and dismissed a large number of soldiers so that our progress would not be slow. My army at the time of entering India numbered 15,000, of which 2,000 were cavalrymen. Before I died at the age of 33, I also built the city of Alexandria in Egypt.

Alexander the Great

Alexander ruled for only 13 years. He was taken ill after a feast in Babylon. After a 10-day fever, Alexander died in the **Palace of Nabukodonossor**. His friends asked: 'To whom do you leave the kingdom?'
He replied: 'To the best.' These were his last words. Predicca received his ring, as the symbol of his regency, before he died.

I was born in the Maurya dynasty in India some time before 300 BC. I ruled the kingdom of **Magadha** from 273 BC to 232 BC. My empire included almost all of what is India today (except the southern tip and the north-eastern part of India). I also had in my empire the territory that today constitutes Pakistan, Bangladesh and part of Afghanistan. My grandfather was **Chandragupta Maurya**. As a prince, I was appointed governor of Vidisa where I married a rich merchant's daughter.

While in Vidisa, I heard that my father was on his deathbed. I hurried to the capital of our kingdom, **Pataliputra**. I occupied the throne and being very ruthless in those days, I killed all the rival princes with the exception of my own brother. I was one of the first royal patrons of Buddhism. After 20 years of my reign, I visited the Buddha's birthplace at Lumbini in modern-day Nepal. Here I put up a pillar recording my visit.

In a remarkable change from my earlier manner, I preached tolerance towards all religions and sent peace missions to countries like Greece, Kandhar, Kashmir, Mysore, Ceylon, Burma, Malaya and Sumatra. My son, Mahendra, and daughter, Sanghamitra, went on a mission to Ceylon. Their visit is celebrated in Sri Lanka to this day. Eight years after I ascended the throne, I invaded **Kalinga**, a kingdom represented by modern-day Orissa.

My war against that kingdom killed thousands of people in battle whilst many thousands died from the effects of the war. As I sat there in the battlefield and looked around me, I was horrified by the killing and bloodshed all around. Women cried for their dead husbands, children wept, and here and there I could see a half dead man raising his arm from the sea of dead people. I renounced killing and wars.

Asoka the Great

In 1837, James Prinsep deciphered an ancient inscription issued by a king calling himself '*Devapriya* or Beloved-of-the-gods, King Priyadasi'. More edicts by this king were discovered and it was finally recognised that King Priyadasi and King Asoka were the same. This was confirmed when, in 1915, another edict actually mentioning the name Asoka was discovered.

I belong to the Ch'in Empire and ascended the throne when I was just 13-years old. I succeeded in uniting China for the first time in history. I introduced a centralised government in China, conducted a census, and standardised the country's coinage, written language, laws, and weights and measures. A network of roads and canals was laid down.

On the downside, I was an authoritarian despot who put in all efforts to stamp out Confucianism. I was only partially successful. I ordered my chancellor to burn all the literary classics of the past. My autocratic rule and belief in magic was what eventually led to the collapse of the Ch'in dynasty, four years later. Ch'in however, formed the model for all later dynasties. In the history of China, I am known as the First Emperor.

On my death, I was buried in great splendour with 6,000 terracotta soldiers to protect me in my afterlife. Ch'in was one of the 'warring states' of China. In 221 BC I annexed all the states that rivalled Ch'in and this was when I took the title of First Emperor. My original name was King Cheng. It is said that the other six states were crushed by me 'as a silkworm devours a mulberry leaf'. In political matters, I was counselled by Li Ssu.

In order to consolidate my rule and protect China from the **Mongols** of Central Asia, I ordered the construction of the **Great Wall of China**. Many emperors from different dynasties contributed to the building of the wall after me. This massive wall eventually stretched 1,500 miles (2,250 km). It was this wall that made it possible for my single, unified China to survive.

Shih Huang Ti

Shih Huang Ti constructed his own tomb which took his entire life for completion. He wanted to take the power and rare treasures accumulated during his life into the next world after his death. His tomb was a fantastic underground palace in which he was buried. This was covered with a huge burial mound.

I was born into a Bania (Vaish or trading caste) family at Kathiawar in Rajkot. I was the youngest of the three sons of my father and his fourth wife Putlibai. Though India was then under British rule, over 500 kingdoms, principalities, and states were allowed autonomy in domestic and internal affairs. These were the so-called 'native states'. Rajkot was one such state.

I got married when I was 14-years old. I went to England in 1882 to study law. In London, I was greatly attracted to theosophists and vegetarians. It was here that I was introduced to the ***Bhagwad Gita***, a book that continued to inspire me throughout my life. After completing my law, I was enrolled in the High Court of London. I, however, returned to India and practised in Bombay (now Mumbai) from 1891 to 1893. I practised law in South Africa until 1914.

In Natal, I became the first Indian to be enrolled as an advocate of the Supreme Court. I returned to India in 1915, and never left the country again except for a short trip to Europe in 1931. I followed the advice of Gokhale, and travelled widely across the country for one year to become familiar with the real India. I was involved in numerous local struggles, such as that at Champaran in Bihar, where workers on indigo plantations complained of the oppressive working conditions.

I stopped wearing a suit and tie and instead, opted for clothes that the poorest of India's people could wear. I preached simplicity and urged my followers to weave their own cloth. I vowed that I would not return to **Sabarmati Ashram** in Ahmedabad, which was then my beloved home, till India attained her independence. In the mid-1930s, I established myself in a remote village called Sevagram. Rabindranath Tagore named me literally as the great soul.

Mahatma Gandhi

My Experiments with Truth is his magnificient autobiography that gives us an insight into the Mahatma. He advocated non-violence, and at the same time promoted the idea of non-cooperation with the British rulers. One example is his 1930 boycott to protest against the imposition of British tax on salt. On January 30,1948, he was assassinated by a Hindu fanatic named Nathuram Godse.

I was the son of a nobleman. I entered the Roman army, and served in Asia with distinction. I received the civic Crown, the highest medal for valour. When I returned to Rome, I entered politics, became state treasurer at the age of 34, chief priest at 39 and was elected to consulship at age 43. My most famous words are: *Veni, vidi, vici*: 'I came, I saw, I conquered.'

Between 58 and 55 BC, I conquered Gaul (France), Helvetii (Switzerland) and Belgica (Belgium). I also invaded and got most of Britain. I crossed the River Rhine to fight the Germans. After I returned to Rome as conquerer of the world, I landed in a political conflict with Pompey, the Roman General who had captured Jerusalem.

I was a General and though we had armies under us, Generals were not allowed to bring their armies into the city of Rome. I broke this rule in order to dispose of Pompey, making myself an absolute ruler. After I consolidated Roman rule over Greece and led a campaign of conquest into Syria and Egypt, I came back to Rome as the **monarch**.

My relationship with Cleopatra is well-renowned. My wars with Gaul have been immortalised in the **Asterix comic books**. I do not know whether Shakespeare is famous because of me or whether I am famous because of him. I was assassinated in a coup led by Brutus in the Roman Senate on March 15, 44 BC. My last words were thus: "*Et tu, Brutus*?" By the time I died, Rome had become the world's first superpower.

Julius Caesar

Roman biographer, Suetonius, wrote thus on Julius Caesar's appearance: He was tall, fair, and well-built. His health was sound, except for the sudden epileptic seizures he was prone to. His baldness was teased by his enemies; but he used to comb the thin strands of hair forward, and of all the honours bestowed on him, none pleased him so much as the privilege of wearing a laurel wreath on all occasions—he constantly took advantage of it.

In the late 1100s and early 1200s, I created a confederation of tribes, called Mongol. It comprised however, of both Mongols and non-Mongols. I was a good manager, and had a number of talented people with me. I was the adopted son of the Mongol Khan, Ong. When I succeeded my father, I got the title of 'Universal Ruler'. I took my title very seriously and set out on a campaign of conquest that lasted 25 years. My original name was Temujin.

In 1202, my forces fought and defeated the **Tartars**. The men who survived, I ordered to be killed, and the women and children were mixed with the other tribes. After the Tartars, I invaded China. It was an easy target for me. I captured Beijing in 1214 and soon occupied most of China. My empire soon became one of the biggest in the world. It stretched from northern China to the Black Sea.

Apart from everything else, the good thing that I did was to make people at opposite ends of the globe know one another. Before the Mongols, the Europeans were largely unaware that the Far East existed. My 'Mongol hordes', as my armies were known, swept over Russia, Persia, Poland and Hungary, giving the people little chance to retaliate.

When I was about 65-years old, in 1227, I fell off my horse while fighting against the Tangut in north-western China. I did not survive the fall. If you look at the extent of my empire, I am the greatest conqueror of all times; yes, even greater than Alexander the Great. Even after I died, the Mongol nation continued to believe that I would rise from death and lead my people to new victories.

Genghis Khan

According to a writer, when invading prosperous cities such as Bukhara (now Uzbekistan) and Samarkand, Genghis Khan told the Muslims, "I am the punishment of God. If you had not committed great sins, God would not have sent punishment like me upon you."

I was born in 1732 into a Virginia planter family. In 1758, after I was elected to the Virginia House of Burgesses, I first became aware of the deep resentment that the Americans had about living in a British colony. During the **American War of Independence**, I was Commander-in-Chief of the Continental Army, whose victory was vital for independence of the 13 colonies. On July 3, 1775, at Cambridge, Massachusetts, I commandeered my ill-trained troops to a war that lasted six years.

After the war, I went back to my home at Mount Vernon in Virginia. However, in 1787, I presided over the Constitutional Convention in Philadelphia. I was the main force behind the drafting of the American constitution, which continues today as the oldest written constitution in the world. I did not infringe upon the policy-making powers that I felt the Constitution gave the Congress. I laid emphasis on foreign policies. In the major war between France and England, during the French Revolution, I insisted upon a neutral course.

I held a contest for designing a 'President's Palace' which was won by an Irish architect named James Hoban. Today the 'palace' is called simply the 'White House'. When I was young, my father gave me a hatchet. I tried to cut down a cherry tree with it. My father, noticing the cuts on the tree, asked me how they got there. "I cannot tell a lie," I said, "I did it with my hatchet." Today in USA, my birthday is celebrated with cherry pies.

In 1789, under the provision of the United States constitution, I was elected by the **Electoral College** as the first President of United States. Re-elected in 1793, I built a strong central government, but one which was governed by consensus of state representatives. I, however, did not have a chance of staying in the White House. I died on December 14, 1799, one year before the White House was completed.

George Washington

George Washington died in December 14, 1799. He was known as the father of his country, and upon his death, the memorial address presented on behalf of the Congress of the United States named him "the first in war, the first in peace, and the first in the hearts of his countrymen."

I was born on February 12, 1809, in a log cabin in Kentucky. My father was a carpenter and farmer. Both my parents were members of a **Baptist** congregation, which had separated from another church due to opposition to slavery. I loved to read and preferred learning to working in the fields. My father was against all this learning as he considered it useless. I was constantly borrowing books from my neighbours.

In 1830, my family moved to Illinois, where I lived until 1837. I had a number of jobs. I looked after a store, I was a surveyor and also a postmaster. In 1834 I was elected to the Illinois state legislature, where I served till 1843. I became a lawyer in 1837 and was elected to the US House of Representatives in 1846. I served one term before returning to Illinois to practise law.

I spoke out against slavery openly without shame or fear. My interest in politics was renewed when the **Kansas-Nebraska Act** was passed in 1854. Though I did not succeed initially, I finally won the presidential elections. I thus became the 16th President of the United States. In February 1861, my family and I came to Washington to stay at the White House. At the suggestion of an 11-year-old girl, I took to wearing a beard.

My years as the President are known for the Civil War that raged over four years. I am remembered for the role I played as a leader of the Union during the Civil War and for beginning the process that led to end of slavery in the United States. On April 14, 1865, while watching the play *Our American Cousin* at Ford's Theatre, I was shot in the back of my head. This was the first case of assassination of a President in American history.

Abraham Lincoln

Lincoln's Gettysburg address is perhaps one of the most famous speeches. It was for the dedication of the military cemetery at Gettysburg. He vowed "that this nation, under God, shall have a new birth of freedom; and that the government of the people, by the people and for the people, shall not perish from the earth."

Born on November 30,1874 at Blenheim Palace, outside Woodstock, I was educated at **Harrow** and at the **Sandhurst Royal Military College**. I served in the British army for six years, distinguishing myself in 1899 during the Boer War in South Africa. I was posted in India and the Sudan, and acted off duty as a war correspondent. I became most notable for my outspoken opposition towards the granting of independence to India. I won the Nobel Prize for literature.

I left the army to join politics but first became a journalist in South Africa. Taken prisoner by the Boers, I made a daring escape. I was elected to Parliament in 1900, and as the first Lord of the Admiralty in 1911, I was responsible for modernisation of the British fleet. This move proved a vital factor in my country's naval successes in First World War. I was blamed for the failure of the Dardanelles campaign in 1915. I quickly returned to British-controlled South Africa where I joined a South African cavalry regiment and was involved in a number of brutal and bloody battles.

When Adolf Hitler invaded Poland on September 1, 1939, and started Second World War, Britain and France declared war. Prime Minister Neville Chamberlain gave me my job back at the Admiralty. In May 1940, Chamberlain resigned and I took his place as the Prime Minister. My speeches were a great inspiration to the embattled United Kingdom. My first speech as Prime Minister was the famous "I have nothing to offer but blood, toil, tears, and sweat" speech.

France surrendered on June 22. Asking the **House of Commons** for vote of confidence in the small war cabinet, I said, "I have nothing to offer but blood, toil, tears and sweat." I warned Hitler that his troops would meet relentless opposition "on the beaches, on the streets and in every village", for which the people loved me. My characteristic trademarks were my hat and my cigar.

Sir Winston Churchill

In 1945, Churchill's Conservative Party was turned out of office, but he returned as Prime Minister in 1951 and served until 1955. Shortly afterwards he was knighted; he suffered a stroke, which considerably slowed him down. He died on January 24, 1965. One of his well-known quotes was: "I am prepared to meet my Maker. Whether my Maker is prepared for the great ordeal of meeting me is another matter."

Born in 1917, I spent a part of my childhood in Allahabad, in our family home, and a part in Switzerland. I received my college education at Somerville College, Oxford, and later went to Rabindranath Tagore's Shantiniketan. As the leader of the monkey brigade (*Vanar Sena*), a children's group working for Independence alongside the Congress, I delivered speeches as a diversion while the other children informed the person who was to be arrested by the British.

After India became independent, I took charge of running the official residence of my father, who was now a widower. I also accompanied him on his numerous trips, within and outside the country. In 1938, I officially joined the Indian National Congress. I got married in 1942; my husband died in 1960. I had two sons, both of whom were fond of flying aircraft. In 1964, the year of my father's death, I was elected to Parliament for the first time.

I became the Minister of Information and Broadcasting in the government of the then Prime Minister, Lal Bahadur Shastri. He died unexpectedly of a heart attack less than two years after assuming office. I was the first woman Prime Minister of India in 1966-77 and was re-elected on 1980-84. It was as if I had always been in politics. *Garibi Hatao* (remove poverty) was my favourite slogan during the election campaigns. I did not like dissent.

I used the army to resolve internal disputes. The first nuclear test at **Pokhran** in 1974 was successfully tested during my period. After India's victory in the war of 1971 against Pakistan, I gained tremendous popularity but by 1973, people demonstrated against inflation and corruption. In June 1975, the High Court of Allahabad found me guilty of using illegal practices during my election campaign. I then declared a state of Emergency.

Indira Gandhi

In her attempt to crush the secessionist movement of Sikh militants, led by Jarnail Singh Bhindranwale, Mrs Indira Gandhi ordered an assault upon the holy Sikh shrine at Amritsar, the Golden Temple. This operation was called Operation Bluestar. The Golden Temple was damaged, and Mrs Gandhi was assassinated in October 1984, the same year, by two of her own Sikh bodyguards. At her death, her elder son, Rajiv Gandhi became the Prime Minister of the country.

I was born in Syracuse on the island of Sicily and studied science under Conon of Samos at the University of Alexandria, which was then considered a world centre for learning. My father was Phidias, an astronomer. There is nothing else known about Phidias other than this one fact. This is all that I could inform about my father through one of my writings, *The Sandreckoner.*

When the Romans attacked Syracuse in 214 BC, I designed a number of useful defence weapons, ranging from long-range catapults to mirrors that used the sun to set fire to the Roman ships. A Roman footsoldier was interfering with some calculations that I was sketching on the ground with a stick, when I shouted at him. The soldier killed me on the spot. When the Roman General, Marcellus, heard what had happened, he erected a tomb in my honour.

I had once said: "Give me a lever long enough and a place to stand, and I will move the world." *The Sandreckoner* is a remarkable work in which I divulge a number system capable of expressing numbers up to 8×1016 in modern notation. I argue in this work that this number is large enough to count the number of grains of sand that could be fitted into the Universe. I also give the dimensions of the Universe in this book.

I devised many of the basic theorems involving the geometry of circles, cones, cylinders, parabolas, planes, and spheres, which constitute the basic building blocks of mathematics. I also invented the science of hydrostatics, which is the study of fluid dynamics. Relaxing in my bathtub, I had once rushed out stark naked, shouting "**Eureka**, Eureka..." One of my most important mechanical inventions was a screw.

Archimedes

In the preface to *On Spirals*, Archimedes says that he used to send his friends' statements of his latest theorems, but, without giving proofs. Apparently, some of the mathematicians claimed the results as their own, so, on the last occasion when he sent them his theorems, Archimedes very cleverly included two theorems, that were false.

A painting by Jusepe de Ribera at Museo del Prado, Spain.

I was born in England in Lincolnshire. I entered Cambridge University in 1661. In 1667, when I was 25, I was elected a Fellow of Trinity College, and Lucasian Professor of Mathematics in 1669. Between 1665 to 1667, I wrote *Philosophiae Naturalis Principia Mathematica*, commonly known as *Principia*, which was published in 1687. I demonstrated the structure of the Universe, the planetary movements, and calculated the mass of the sun, the planets and their moon.

I invented the binomial theorem and functional calculus, and discovered the spectrum of light before the age of 24. I also invented the reflector telescope, which differed from the simpler refractor type invented by Hans Lippershey. I made contributions to all branches of mathematics then studied, but became especially famous for my solutions to problems in analytical geometry of drawing tangents to curves (differentiation) and defining areas bounded by curves (integration).

In 1696 I moved to London as Warden of the **Royal Mint**. I became Master of the Mint in 1699 and continued as such till my death. I served in the English Parliament from 1701 to 1705, and was knighted by Queen Anne in 1705. I served as president of the Royal Society from 1703 until my death at Kensington. I was re-elected every year.

It was while I was at Cambridge that I developed my **Three Laws of Motion**. I conceived the gravitational force, while watching an apple fall around the year 1665. I calculated the force needed to hold the Moon in its orbit, as compared with the force pulling an object to the ground. I also calculated the centripetal force needed to hold a stone in a sling, and the relation between the length of a pendulum and the time of its swing.

Sir Isaac Newton

Newton was a modest man of simple tastes. He had more books on humanities than on mathematics and science. Newton left a mass of manuscripts on subjects like alchemy and chemistry, then closely related topics. Both in the government and at the Royal Society, he proved an able administrator. He never married and lived modestly. He was buried with great pomp in Westminster Abbey.

I was born in Shrewsbury, England as the fifth child and second son of Robert Waring and Susannah Wedgwood. I was educated at Cambridge, where I took particular interest in science in general and the evolution of the natural world, in particular. Immediately after graduating from Cambridge, I accepted a position as an unpaid naturalist on a five-year survey expedition abroad the vessel '*HMS Beagle*'.

For five years, the ship's crew surveyed South America, Australia, New Zealand and countless islands. In South America I found fossils of extinct animals that were similar to modern species. On Galapagos Islands in the Pacific Ocean I noticed many variations among plants and animals of the same general type as those in South America. Upon my return to London, I conducted thorough research of my notes and specimens.

Out of this study grew several related theories: one, evolution did occur; two, evolutionary change was gradual, requiring thousands to millions of years; three, the primary mechanism for evolution was a process called natural selection; and four, the millions of species alive today arose from a single original life form through a branching process called 'specialisation'.

This gave birth to my theory of evolutionary selection which says that variation within species occurs randomly and the survival or extinction of each organism is determined by that organism's ability to adapt to its environment. I wrote about these theories in my book called, *The Origin of Species* in 1859. In 1871, I published *The Descent of Man*, in which I expressed the controversial theory that man had evolved from a non-human ancestor, the ape.

Charles Darwin

Many people strongly opposed the idea of evolution because it conflicted with their religious convictions. Shortly after Darwin's death, an evangelist claimed she visited Darwin at his death-bed, when he said he no longer believed in evolution. This story was refuted by Darwin's daughter who stated, "I was present at his death-bed. . . He never recanted any of his scientific views, either then or earlier."

I was born to Chandrasekhara Ayer and Parvathi Ammal in the town called Tiruchirapalli in Tamil Nadu, on November 7, 1888. At the age of 11, I passed out from secondary school and entered A.V.N. College. Two years later I moved to Presidency College in Madras. In 1905, I was the only boy who passed in first class with honours in physics and English. I then took up physics as my subject for M.A. in the same college. In 1907, barely 17, I post-graduated to top my class with honours.

I joined the Indian Civil Services as an Assistant Accountant General in Calcutta. In my spare time, I worked in laboratories of the Indian Association for Cultivation of Science. I studied the science behind stringed instruments and Indian drums. Works of the German scientist Helmhotlz and the English scientist Lord Raleigh on acoustics greatly influenced me. When I was 18-years old, one of my research papers was published in the *Philosophical Magazine* of England.

In 1917, I was offered the position of Sir Taraknath Palit Professorship in physics at Calcutta University, where I stayed for the next 15 years. During my tenure, I received worldwide recognition for my work in optics and scattering of light. I was elected to the Royal Society of London in 1924 and knighted in 1929. In 1928 the Science Society of Rome awarded the Matteucci Medal to me. In 1930, I became the first Indian as also the first Asian to receive the Nobel Prize for physics.

On February 28, 1928, I observed two low-intensity spectral lines corresponding to the incident monochromatic light. It became famous as the '**Raman Effect**'. This confirmed that light was made up of particles known as photons and this helped in the study of molecular and crystal structures. In 1947, I was appointed the first national professor of Independent India. In 1934, I became Director of the newly-established Indian Institute of Sciences in Bangalore. I also received the **Bharat Ratna**.

C. V. Raman

Professor Eliot of Presidency College, Madras, saw a little boy in his B.A. class. Thinking that the boy had strayed into the room, the professor asked, "Are you a student of the B.A. class?"
"Yes, sir,"
"Your name?"
"C.V. Raman."
This made the 14-year old boy well known. He established the Raman Research Institute at Bangalore, and remained active in research until his death on November 21, 1970, at the age of 82.

I was born on October 11, 1942 in Allahabad, India. I studied at Sherwood College in Nainital where my acting skills first surfaced. I continued participating in plays while studying at Delhi's Kirori Mal College. I earned a double M.A. degree. My father was one of the most famous poets of India. I was earlier a stage actor, radio announcer and freight company executive in Calcutta.

My struggle in the Mumbai film industry was long and I had to face rejection initially. I was considered too tall, too dark, and too thin to be a leading star. I gave up my film career in the nineties to join politics and even won the Allahabad Parliament seat. I however, failed to make a mark in politics. K.A. Abbas gave me my first break in *Saat Hindustani*. The film failed to make an impact at the box-office.

I continued to struggle, and even played the role of a mute in *Reshma aur Shera*. There were some more flops; in one film, *Parwana*, I also played the role of a villain with Navin Nischol as the hero (1971). I got the award for the best supporting actor in Hindi film *Anand* (1972), but my performance was eclipsed by a superb one from Rajesh Khanna.

Then came *Zanjeer*. I actually got the lead role in the film because all the stars refused to play the part which I took up as a challenge. The film became a superhit and I became a star. This was the beginning of my career as the 'angry young man'. I blasted my way to box-office success and into India's heart. I had my revenge against Rajesh Khanna by outshining him in *Namak Haraam* (1974), which got me the award for Best Supporting Actor.

Amitabh Bachchan

Amitabh was chosen as the Superstar of the Millennium over Charlie Chaplin and Lawrence Olivier on a BBC online poll. He is the first filmstar from India to be represented at **Madame Tussaud's Wax Museum**, London. His television series *Kaun Banega Crorepati* make thousands sit glued to their television, 9 o'clock every evening. In 2001 he was awarded the Padma Bhushan for his contribution to Indian cinema.

I am known as the father of modern classical music and am said to be one of the most prolific geniuses in the history of western music. I spent my entire life in Germany, writing, teaching and performing music. I was the youngest son of a town musician, from whom I am said to have learnt the violin and the rudiments of musical theory. Orphaned at the age of 10, I went to live with my brother as an organist in nearby Ohrdruf.

In 1708, I became an organist and chamber musician to the Duke of Saxe-Weimar. In 1717, I was appointed **Kapellmeister** at Cöthen. I was at first refused permission to leave Weimar and was allowed to do so only after being held prisoner by the Duke for almost a month. I spent six years as the court conductor for Prince Leopold of Anhalt-Cothen. It was here that I had the opportunity to write some of the works for which I am held in awe today.

In 1723, I accepted a post at the Thomas Schule School in Leipzig and remained there for life. I produced an amazing number of cantatas, fugues, chorales and other compositions. During my early years in Leipzig, I composed church music, including four or five cantata cycles, the *Magnificat* and the *St. John* and *St. Matthew Passions*. From about 1729, my interest in church music declined, and most of my later works, like *Minor Mass* and the *Christmas Oratorio*, imitated my earlier music.

My six **Brandenburg concertos** for chamber orchestra, composed while with Prince Leopold, are among the leading masterpieces of classical music. At Potsdam, after my children had grown up, I improvised on a theme given to me by the king. This developed into a composition of the *Musical Offering*, a compendium of fugue, canon, and sonata based on the royal theme.

Johann Sebastian Bach

Bach composed over 1,000 works. Dr Wolfgang Schmieder compiled a numerical listing of Bach according to musical forms. He assigned a BWV number (Bach Werk Verzeichnis) to each work, and this idea was so successful, that most of Bach's works are now known not only through their title, but also through their BWV number.

I was born on 27th June 1880 in Tuscumbia, a small rural town in northwest Alabama, USA. I had a modest upbringing. My father, Captain Arthur Henley Keller, worked as a cotton plantation owner and as an editor of a weekly local newspaper. I was born with full sight and hearing but when I was less than two-years old I fell violently ill. This mysterious illness left me both blind and deaf.

On Alexander Graham Bell's suggestion, my parents requested the director of the Perkins Institution and Massachusetts Asylum for the Blind, to find a teacher for me. He recommended Anne Sullivan, a former pupil of the institution. She taught me to finger spell and also attempted to control my increasingly bad behaviour. A trip to the water pump on April 5, 1887, changed my life. My teacher placed my hand under the cool gush of water and in the other hand she spelt the word "water", first slowly, then rapidly. That's when the mystery of language was revealed.

I joined the Cambridge School for Young Ladies in 1896 and entered the Radcliffe College in the autumn of 1900. With this, I became the first deaf and blind person to have ever taken admission in an institution of higher learning. I published my first book *The Story of My Life* in 1903 that later became a classic. I wrote *The World I Live In*, revealing my thoughts on my world for the first time. In 1909, I became a member of the Socialist Party of Massachusetts.

I conducted extensive fund-raising tours for the American Foundation for the Blind. I also campaigned tirelessly to alleviate the living and working conditions of blind people who were usually badly educated and living in asylums. After Second World War, I travelled to Japan, Australia, South America, Europe and Africa to raise funds for the American Foundation for the Overseas Blind. *The Miracle Worker*, a drama portraying my teacher's first success in communicating with me as a child, went on to become a hit Broadway play and then later was made into a film.

Helen Adams Keller

Helen Keller was once asked as to how disabled veterans of Second World War should be treated and she replied that they do "not want to be treated as heroes. They want to be able to live naturally and to be treated as human beings." She was a tireless activist for racial and gender equality.

I was born in Portsmouth, England, to a naval pay clerk and his wife Elizabeth Barrow. My early years were an idyllic time. I have described myself as a "very small and not-over-particularly-taken-care-of boy". I spent my time in the outdoors, reading voraciously. I had extremely strong memories of childhood and photographic memory of people and events that helped bring my fiction to life. My father was imprisoned for running into debt and at the age of 12, I began working for 10 hours a day in Warren's boot-blacking factory.

I spent my time pasting labels on the jars of thick polish and earned six shillings a week. With this money I had to pay for my lodging and help support my family who were **incarcerated** in the nearby Marshalsea debtors' prison. After a few years my family's financial situation improved but I never forgave my mother for my plight and conditions of the working-class people became major themes of my works. I wrote, "No advice, no counsel, no encouragement, no consolation, no support from anyone that I can call to mind, so help me God!"

In May 1827 I began work as a law clerk, then a journalist, reporting parliamentary debate and travelling around Britain by stagecoach to cover election campaigns. In my early 20s, I made a name for myself with my first novel, *The Pickwick Papers*. On April 2, 1836 I married Catherine Hogarth, with whom I had ten children. I separated from her in 1858, because she did not share quite the same boundless energy for life as I possessed.

I wrote many novels, among which *David Copperfield, Great Expectations, Oliver Twist, A Tale of Two Cities* became famous. I used my rich imagination, sense of humour and detailed memories, particularly of my childhood to enliven my writing. On June 9, 1870, I died. The inscription on my tomb reads: "He was a sympathiser to the poor, the suffering, and the oppressed; and by his death, one of England's greatest writers is lost to the wrold."

Charles Dickens

Charles John Huffam Dickens (1812 -1870), was a cherished English novelist of the Victorian era. The popularity of his novels and short stories during his lifetime and to the present is demonstrated by the fact that none of his novels has ever gone out of print. His writing style was poetic and florid with a strong comic touch.

I was born to Vernon and Gladys in a two-room house in Tupelo, Mississippi on January 8, 1935. I and my parents moved to Memphis, Tennessee in 1948, and I graduated from Humes High School in 1953. I was highly influenced by pop and country music, gospel music, and the black R&B. I was a truck driver when I made my first recording. In 1954, I began my singing career with the legendary Sun Records label in Memphis. In late 1955, my recording contract was sold to RCA Victor.

By 1956, I became an international sensation. I influenced many other top-name artists such as the Beatles. I served in the army between 1958 and 1960 stationed in Germany. Graceland, my home and refuge for 20 years, is one of the most visited homes in America today, now attracting over 600,000 visitors annually. It is also the most famous home in America after the White House. In 1991, Graceland Mansion was placed at the National Register of Historic Places.

Soon I was dancing before hysterical crowds. By 1956, I released hits like *Heartbreak Hotel* and *Hound Dog*. I starred in 31 successful feature films and two documentaries. My American sales earned me gold, platinum or multi-platinum awards for 140 different albums and singles, far more than any other artist. Among my many awards were 14 Grammy nominations (three wins), and the Grammy Lifetime Achievement Award, which I got at 36.

I died at my Memphis home, Graceland, on August 16, 1977 from an accidental drug overdose. Globally, I have sold over one billion records, the highest of any recording artist to date. My sideburns and clothes have a unique style, copied by many. Every year at my death anniversary, millions organise shows with my look-alikes. I am the undisputed king of 'rock and roll', and it appears that I have become much more popular after my death.

Elvis Presley

Elvis Presley's trophy room at Graceland is filled with gold and platinum records and awards of all kinds from all over the world. The three Grammies he won were for two gospel recordings—*How Great Thou Art* (1967), *He Touched Me* (1972) and his live Memphis concert recording of *How Great Thou Art* (1974).

I was born on April 15, 1452, in the small Tuscan town of Vinci, near Florence. I was the son of a wealthy Florentine notary and a peasant woman. I was given the basics of schooling in my father's house. I was handsome, could talk with conviction, was a fine musician and improviser. My fascination with machines began when I was still a boy.

In 1467, at the age of 14, I was apprenticed as a *garzone*, or studio boy, to Andrea Del Verrocchio, a leading painter and sculptor in Florence. I was taught the fundamentals of painting and how to complete works for altar pieces and panel pictures, as well as the creation of marble and bronze structures. By the time I was 20, I was introduced into the painters' guild, and became an independent master six years later.

My first commission was to paint an altarpiece for the chapel of the Palazzo Vecchio. This was never done. My first large painting, *The Adoration of the Magi*, was left unfinished, but is unique. I then wrote a letter to the Duke of Milan in which I said that I could construct a portable bridge, catapults, cannons and armoured vehicles. Thus I entered the world of the royalty and remained there for 17 years. I also assisted the Italian mathematician Luca Pacioli in his famous work, *Divina Proportione*.

The most important of my paintings during the early **Milan period** was *The Virgin of the Rocks*, two versions of which exist. It was at this time that I developed my unique style and worked on what was to be my masterpiece, *The Last Supper*. I returned to Florence and was employed by Cesare Borgia, Duke of Romagna, as chief architect and engineer in 1502. Here I painted my most recognised painting, ***Mona Lisa***, also known as *La Gioconda*, as it was presumed to be her last name.

Leonardo da Vinci in the background with his famous *Mona Lisa* painting in inset.

Leonardo da Vinci

The ***Last Supper*** is a mural in the monastery of Santa Maria delle Grazie, Milan. Leonardo experimented with the use of oil on dry plaster, which was technically unsound, and by 1500 its deterioration had begun. A restoration and conservation programme is underway to restore it. He drew his mechanical ideas with exceptional clarity. Five hundred years after they were put on paper, many of his sketches can easily be used as blueprints to create perfect working models.

I was born on September 28, 1929 at Indore in Madhya Pradesh state. My father was a classical singer and stage actor from Goa. He was trained in the colourful Punjabi school of Baba Mushelkar. We children, his four daughters and a son, did not receive proper schooling. However to compensate for this, we were given music lessons early in life. Besides my father, I studied with Aman Ali Khan Sahib and later Amanat Khan.

I acted in films till I was 15. I even took up small roles as an extra because I had to support my younger siblings. I first sang as a playback singer for a Marathi film in 1942 but it was not used however. My first playback song was thus *Pahili Mangalagaur.* My first song as a playback singer in Hindi films was in 1947 – *Aapki Sewa Mein.* I was still unknown till Ghulam Haider heard me and took me to Subodh Mukherjee. Ghulam Haider gave me my first major song: *Dil mera toda* from *Majboor* in 1948.

I won the first Flimfare Award for the Best Playback Singer for *Madhumati* (*Aajare pardesi*) in 1958. I was the star amongst the playback singers till the end of the 1990s. I got the best of the music world from leading music directors of the time: Laxmikant Pyarelal, R.D. Burman and Kalyanji Anandji. Starting off with a Royal Albert Hall concert in London, my live shows too increased.

I am single and am married to music. Even today, as I enter a recording room, I remove my *chappals* because this is where Goddess Saraswati resides. I have an avid interest in cricket and am an admirer of Sachin Tendulkar. A white sari and a single plait have always been my trademark. The *Guinness Book of Records* listed me as the most recorded artist in the world with 30,000 solo, duet and chorus-backed songs recorded in 20 Indian languages between 1948 and 1987.

Lata Mangeshkar

Lata has won the Dadasaheb Phalke Award and the Bharat Ratna. It was always the co-singers, be it Mohammad Rafi or Mukesh who dispite their differences came back to her. She has another side to her; she apparently never charged a paisa from Yash Chopra for singing in his films. She did it absolutely free.

I was the oldest of six children of a **Protestant** minister in Groot Zundert, Holland. Born on March 30, 1853, I was a moody, restless, and temperamental boy. At the same time, I was also articulate and well read. This could well be gauged from the more than 700 letters that I wrote to my brother Theo. At 16, I was sent to the Hague, Holland, to work for my uncle, a partner in an international firm of art dealers, where I studied painting with Anton Mauve.

As I did not do much to attract and retain clients, I was transferred to the London branch, and then sent from uncle to uncle. I worked as a schoolmaster in England. I had by now decided to become a clergyman and began training for the *ministry* at Amsterdam University. I enrolled for evangelical training in Belgium, but I soon left this and worked as a preacher among the poor coal-miners there. At 27 years of age, I realised I was born to be an artist.

After spending two years in the countryside of Brabant, I moved back to Holland, where I painted *The Potato Eaters.* At the end of 1885, I joined the academy of art in Antwerp, Belgium. The teacher told me that my strokes were too heavy and I left the academy on the second day itself. Moving to Paris in 1886, I gave up my bold brush strokes and moralistic realism. I moved to Arles in the south of France, in 1888, hoping to establish an artists' colony there.

The colours of the Mediterranean stunned me and my paintings that followed, such as *Sunflowers* (1888), *Night Watch* (1888) and *Starry Night* (1889) were a result of this. In April 1889, I entered the Saint-Paul-de-Mausole asylum as a voluntary patient, producing 150 paintings in one year. My bouts of depression became more acute and I shot myself on July 27, 1890. In my entire life, I managed to sell just one painting, *Red Vineyard at Arles.*

Vincent van Gogh

In Arles, where van Gogh went to rest, he had invited the painter Paul Gauguin to join him. It is rumoured that the two artists had an argument and van Gogh threatened Gauguin with a razor. The same night, feeling remorse for his actions, van Gogh cut off his own ear. The event was commemorated by van Gogh by executing his *Self Portrait with Bandaged Ear* (1889).

One of the most prolific artists in history, I created more than 20,000 oil canvasses in my lifetime. Born on October 25, 1881, in Malaga, Spain to an academic painter, Jose Ruiz Blanco, I began to draw at an early age. I completed my first painting, *Picador*, when I was eight-years old. I have experimented with every medium of art. I feel "the whole world is open before us, everything waiting to be done."

In 1895, my family moved to Barcelona, and I studied at La Lonja, the Academy of Fine Arts. My early artistic ventures can be credited to my visits to Horta de Ebro from 1898 to 1899 and the group at the Café Els Quatre Gats in 1899. My first exhibition took place in Barcelona in 1900. In 1971 my work was exhibited at the Louvre Museum in Paris, making me the only living artist to feature there. I died on April 8, 1973 in Mougins, France.

I was a snob and held women artists in contempt. I felt women were either 'goddesses or doormats'. My daughter, Maria Therese was the model for my painting *Girl Before the Mirror.* In this painting a girl sees herself imperfectly and my use of colour and reflected image will help you look into the emotions of the girl. In 1937, I protested against the World War with my anti-war painting ***Guernica***. Death became a major subject in most of my works from 1939 to 1945.

My style can be divided into periods—Blue Period (1901-04); Rose Period (1905); the painting *Les Demoiselles d'Avignon* (1907); Classical or Cubism Period, which included an analytic phase (1908-11) and a synthetic phase (beginning in 1912-13). Beggars and the street life of Paris were subjects of my Blue Period. Blindness was my theme in *The Old Guitarist* (1903). My famous cubist paintings are *Head of a Woman* (1909) and *The Three Musicians* (1921).

Pablo Picasso

Picasso applied the principle of cubism to sculpture as in *Mandolin and Clarinet.* He introduced the art form known as collage when he pasted an oilcloth to the painting *Still Life in a Chair*. His association with the Communist Party began in 1944. After the synthetic phase, his work was characterised by **neo-classicism** and he developed a renewed interest in drawing.

Born in Calcutta in 1952 to a shoe company executive, and a female judge, I am the oldest of three children. I was sent to Doon School in Dehradun, Uttaranchal, at the age of six. I was a shy boy, but excelled in studies. I took my undergraduate degree in philosophy, politics, and economics from Oxford University, and was a graduate student at Stanford and Nanjing universities, where I studied the economic demography of China.

While at Stanford, I shifted from graduating in economics to master Chinese. During 1980-1982, I studied classical Chinese poetry. After two years at Nanjing University, I hitchhiked home to New Delhi via Tibet. Fluent in Chinese and garbed in the traditional blue trousers, jacket, and visored cap, I recorded my astute observations and candid conversations in a fascinating travelogue, which was published in 1983.

In 1986, while still at Stanford, I wrote a novel entirely in verse called *The Golden Gate*, a story about life in San Francisco. When I was discouraged by friends, who felt a verse book would never sell, instead of getting discouraged, I included them into the text, 'Drivelling in rhyme's all very well/The question is does spittle sell?'

My first novel was on four extended families in post-colonial India in the early 1950s, called *A Suitable Boy* and published in 14 countries; over one million copies were sold worldwide. My works include: *Mappings* (1980), *From Heaven Lake* (1983), *The Golden Gate* (1986), *All You who Sleep Tonight* (1990), *Beastly Tales from Here to There* (1991), *Three Chinese Poets* (1992), *A Suitable Boy* (1993), *Arion and the Dolphin* (1994) and *An Equal Music* (1999).

Vikram Seth

Vikram's brother conducts Buddhist meditation tours and his youngest sister is an Austrian diplomat. His first novel, *A Suitable Boy* contains 1,349 pages—the longest single-volume novel ever published in English. Vikram Seth is reported to have been paid an advance of £ 1.3 million by Time Warner Books for his other book, *Two Lives*—a memoir built around his great uncle Shanti who married a German Jewish girl, Henny, whom he befriended while staying with her family in Berlin in the thirties.

I was born in the Italian city-state of Venice at a time when Europeans had little or no idea of East Asia. In the early 1200s, my father Nicolo and uncle, Maffeo, decided that the best way to learn about China was to go there. My father left my mother to go to China when I was very small. After a long and difficult trek, they were received at the court of Kublai Khan, the Mongol Emperor of China. By the time my father returned, I was 14-years old!

In 1271, my father and uncle decided to return to China, and this time took me along. Kublai Khan liked me and sent me as an ambassador to many places within China and to Tibet and Burma. I saw more of Asia than any European had ever seen. We returned after 20 years but no one believed me when I spoke of eyeglasses, icecream, noodles, and the riches of Asia in Venice. People were quite impressed though, when they were shown the riches that we brought back.

Three years after I returned to Venice, I was captured in a war against Genoa. I spent a year in a Genoese prison, where one of my fellow-prisoners made me dictate the story of my travels. It was published as *The Description of the World*. My description of the wealth of China, the might of the Mongol Empire, and the exotic customs of India and Africa made the book a bestseller soon after. It was also known as *Il Milione* or *The Million Lies*, because only a few believed that my stories were true.

I remained in Venice until my death in 1324 at age 70. At my death-bed, I enjoyed saying: "I have only told the half of what I saw!" I left my family substantial money. Though 30 years had passed, I still owned a substantial quantity of cloths, valuable pieces, coverings, brocades of silk and gold, exactly like those mentioned several times in my book, together with other precious objects. Among these was a golden plaque that was given to me by Kublai Khan when I left the Mongol capital.

Marco Polo

Much of what Marco Polo wrote was confirmed by travellers of the 18th and 19th centuries. Some of the information in his book were incorporated in maps of the late Middle Ages and proved useful to explorers in the next century. According to Henry Yule, the great geographer: "He was the first traveller to trace a route across Asia, naming and describing kingdom after kingdom. . . His work is said to be the precursor of scientific geography."

I was born on May 11, 1904, in the small agricultural town of Figueres, Spain in the foothills of the Pyrenees. Before I was 10-years old, I had completed two paintings, *Joseph Greeting his Brother* and portrait of *Helen of Troy*. I was taught traditional art at a municipal school of art by Juan Nunez, where I experimented with various art forms—from impressionism to pointillism. I have admitted in my autobiography that my life had episodes of violent hysteria.

At the age of 17, I entered the National School of Art in Madrid, where I won several prizes. During my school years, I discovered the writing of psychologist Sigmund Freud, whose theory of the unconscious influenced my later life. I was also influenced by the surrealist artist and writer, especially the poet, Andre Breton. I held numerous exhibitions throughout Spain, and in 1925 had my first solo show.

I used realism in my *Basket of Bread* (1926) and cubism in *Harlequin* (1926). It wasn't until 1927, when I painted *Blood is Sweeter than Honey*, that demonstrated my renowned hallucinatory art. Called mad by many, I have said, "The only difference between me and a mad man is that I am not mad." Throughout my life I cultivated eccentricity and exhibitionism. One of my most famous acts was appearing in a diving suit at the opening of the London Surrealist Exhibition in 1936.

I emerged as a leader of the **surrealist movement** and my painting, *Persistence of Memory* (1931), where limp watches hang from distorted trees, is still one of the best known surrealist works. I produced two films—*An Andalusian Dog* (1928) and *The Golden Age* (1930). In 1974, I opened the Teatro Museo Dali in Figueres. During Second World War, my wife, Gala Eduard and I took refuge in the United States, returning after the war's end, to Spain.

Salvador Dali

Dali's international reputation continued to grow, based on publicity as well as his prodigious output of paintings, graphic works and book illustrations; as also designs for jewellery, textiles, clothing, costumes, shop interiors and stage sets. He continued working until his death on January 23, 1989.

I was born to a middle-class family in Mumbai on the July 10, 1949. My maternal uncle Madhav Mantri played Test cricket for India. I attended St. Xavier's College simply because it had a cricket team with several first-class players, including Ashok Mankad and Kailash Gattani. My mother practised with me when I was a kid. Cricket ran in my family. At the same time, very few know that I also represented my school in table-tennis.

I scored an astonishing 774 runs with an average of 154.80 in my debut series against West Indies, in 1971. After this however, I went through a lean phase. I got over this phase on a personal level during the trip to England in 1974, where I scored a magnificent century at Old Trafford and was recognised as the best batsman against pace bowling. Early in my test career, I had opened the bowling alongwith Eknath Solkar and Abid Ali.

After my retirement in 1987, I put to use my years of experience as a cricketer and became a columnist for some leading newspapers and magazines. I am also a widely respected TV commentator. The immense popularity I enjoy also made me the **Sheriff** of Mumbai in 1994. I still continue to hold sway with my lively and at times acerbic commenting during matches. My charm and charisma has made me a household figure in India.

I scored 34 Test centuries and took 108 catches, making myself the first Indian, apart from wicket-keepers, to reach a landmark of 100 catches. I became the first player to score 10,000 runs when I played a late cut to Ijaz Fakih in the Fourth Test against Pakistan at Ahmedabad. I was, at best, a conservative captain. The highlight of my captaincy was the 2-0 Test series which we won against Pakistan in 1979-80.

Sunil Manohar Gavaskar

Gavaskar would have become a fisherman if it were not for his uncle, Narayan Masurkar, who had noticed a hole in his left ear-lobe when he had come to see him the day he was born. The next day, when he came again, he saw that the baby did not have the hole on the left ear-lobe. After a frantic search, he was found sleeping peacefully next to a fisherwoman. Gavaskar was then restored to his family.

Writer and humorist, I was one of the most influential and well-loved writers in American literary history. Born in Florida, Missouri, in 1852, I began writing humorous stories for the *Hannibal* journal. After working as a typesetter in various towns, from St. Louis to Cincinnati, Ohio to New York City, I worked for a time as a river-boat pilot. My pen name is adopted from a code name by Mississippi river-men, meaning 'two fathoms down', indicating a particular river channel depth.

Between 1864 and 1867, I worked for several newspapers in San Francisco. Published in 1867, my first book, *The Celebrated Jumping Frog of Calaveras County* was a collection of short stories celebrating life on the western frontier. That same year, I travelled to Europe and the Middle East and later, satirically recounted my observations in the book *Innocent Abroad* (1869). In 1869, I settled in Buffalo, New York, as part owner of a newspaper and married Olivia Langdon in 1870.

In my lifetime, my books were quite successful. In the 1890s I lost most of my earnings in financial speculations and saw the closure of my publishing firm. To recover from bankruptcy, I started a world lecture tour, during which one of my daughters died. This followed by the death of my daughter Susan in 1895 and my wife in 1904 deeply depressed me. I published *Personal Recollections of Joan of Arc* in 1896 and *The Equator* in 1897 which earned me enough money to pay my debts.

My last work, *The Mysterious Stranger*, was finished in 1898 but was published posthumously in 1916. Born as Samuel Clemens, I also wrote *The Prince and the Pauper* (1882) and *A Connecticut Yankee in King Arthur's Court* (1899)—historical novels laced with my characteristic wit and humour. My most famous works include *Life on the Mississippi* (1883), *The Adventures of Tom Sawyer* (1876) and *The Adventures of Huckleberry Finn* (1884).

Mark Twain

Mark Twain (1835-1910) was a humorist, writer and lecturer. After his wife's death (1904), Twain expressed his pessimism about human character in such late works as the posthumously published *Letters from the Earth* (1962).

Traditionally, April 23 is observed as my birthday, and a house on Henley Street in Stratford, owned by my father is accepted as my birthplace. My maternal grandfather, Robert Arden, had a large property, most of which was left to my mother, Mary. My father, John, came to Stratford from Snitterfield before 1532, as an apprentice glover and tanner of leather.

I began my education at the age of six at the Stratford Grammar School, which you can still see. In 1582, I married Anne Hathaway, and our daughter Susanna was born in 1583. Soon after this, we moved to London, where I became a successful actor. I also began to write plays with many ideas in my head. Come to think of it, despite being an outsider to London, it was wonderful how people appreciated my works. Actors and audiences alike enjoyed the plays I wrote.

Because of the plague, the theatres closed down in 1592. I began to write poetry. I returned to the theatre in 1594 as a leading member of the Lord Chamberlain's men. We performed several times in front of Queen Elizabeth I. For these performances we were paid £ 10 each. In 1599, I and my theatre colleagues built the Globe Theatre, then the largest theatre in England. In 1610, I retired to Stratford to write independently as well as with other writers.

Between 1594 and 1603, while I was in my thirties, I wrote 11 of my most famous comedies, including *Two Gentleman of Verona*, *The Taming of the Shrew*, *A Midsummer Night's Dream*, *The Merchant of Venice*, *Much Ado about Nothing*, *As You Like It* and *Twelfth Night*. Three of my greatest works are tragedies and historical plays: *Henry V*, *Julius Caesar*, and *Romeo and Juliet*. The last play that I wrote entirely by myself before my death in 1616 was *The Tempest*.

William Shakespeare

Shakespeare learned his reading and writing skills from an *ABC* or horn-book. Records reveal that his paternal grandfather was a tenant farmer, who was often fined for grazing cattle on common grounds. Shakespeare's father, in an application for a coat of arms, claimed that his grandfather (Shakespeare's great grandfather) was a hero in the **War of the Roses** and was granted land in Warwickshire in 1485 by Henry VII.

I was Emperor of India from 1628 to 1658. I was born in Lahore, Pakistan. My full name was Khurram Shihab-ud-din Muhammad. I rebelled against my father in 1622. I was, however, forgiven and I succeeded to the throne at the age of 35. My father-in-law, Asaf Khan was amongst the many able advisors that I had. I preferred Agra to Delhi as my place of residence.

My reign saw two wars in the Deccan—the subjugation of Bijapur and Golconda, and attacks on the Uzbegs and Persians. I conquered most of the Deccan and temporarily recovered Kandhar from the Persians. My third wife was a Persian princess, whose real name was Arjumand Banu. She passed away after giving birth to our fourteenth child in Burhanpur.

I was a ruthless but able ruler. The magnificence of my court was unequalled. I built a new capital, **Shahjahanabad**, due to scarcity of water in Fatehpur Sikri. I fell seriously ill in 1657, and this led to a war of succession among my sons. In 1658, I was arrested and imprisoned for the rest of my life by my son, Aurangzeb. From the window of my prison, I would sit and watch the tomb of my wife. I was later buried next to her.

Literature flourished at my court. I was the wealthiest of the Mughal rulers. I enjoyed building on a grand scale. Upon my ascension to the throne, I included three major courts in the Agra fort: Diwan-i-Khas and Diwan-i-Aam; Machhi Bhavan; and a residential court called Anguri Bagh. The other monuments that I got built included the Red Fort, the **Taj Mahal**—the tomb of my beloved third wife, Mumtaz Mahal and the **Pearl Mosques** at Agra and Delhi.

Shah Jahan

After his wife's death, Shah Jahan withdrew from materialistic pleasures and gave up all riches of life. He shifted Mumtaz's body from the garden of Zinabad in Burhanpur temporarily to the beautiful gardens of Raja Jai Singh of Amber. For this, he compensated the king by giving him four imperial residences. A huge workforce of 22,000 people worked in completing his dream—the Taj Mahal at a stupendous amount of 32 million rupees at that time.

I was born in Seattle, Washington, on October 28, 1955. I grew up with two sisters. My father was an attorney and mother, a schoolteacher. I attended a public elementary school and the private Lakeside School. It was here I discovered my interest in software and I began programming computers at the age of 13.

During my freshman year at Harvard University, my friend Paul Allen and I became the first persons to adopt a computer language, BASIC, for microcomputers, specifically the MITS Altair computer. In 1975, I dropped out of Harvard and with Allen, moved to Albuqerque, New Mexico, where MITS had its headquarters, and founded a corporation of our own. When MITS closed in 1979, Allen and I returned to the Seattle area to develop software.

In 1980, our corporation was chosen by International Business Machines (IBM) to develop the operating system for its new personal computer. I bought an operating system from a programmer named Tim Paterson and adopted it as MS-DOS. Today, in addition to computers, I am interested in biotechnology. I am on the board of the ICOS Corporation and a shareholder in Chiroscience Group of the United Kingdom and its wholly owned subsidiary, Chiroscience R&D Inc. of Bothell.

Allen retired in 1983 for health reasons. By 1984, our corporation, Microsoft, was doing $100 million worth of business annually, and this doubled in 1986 when its stock was first publicly traded on the New York Stock Exchange. By 1987, with 45 per cent of the stock, I became the computer industry's first billionaire. In the 1990s, I began focusing on graphic user interface system, such as the well-known Windows programme, and on interactive, multimedia systems, such as **CD-ROMs**.

William Henry Gates III

In 1995 Gates wrote *The Road Ahead*—his vision of where the information technology would take society. Co-authored by Nathan Myhrvold, Microsoft's chief technology officer, and Peter Rinearson, *The Road Ahead* sold more than 400,000 copies in China alone.

I was born between August and October 1451, in Genoa, Italy as the eldest son of Domencio Colombo and his wife, Susanna Fontanarossa. In 1479, I married Felipa Perestello e Moniz and our son Diego, was born in 1480. After Felipa died in 1485, I had a second son, Ferdinand, from Beatriz Enriquez de Harana of Cordoba.

I began to navigate at the age of 14. My early voyages were to those ports in the Mediterranean where my countrymen from Genoa frequented. This being too timid for me, I made an excursion to the northern seas (1467), and visited the coasts of Iceland, to which the English and other nations had begun to resort on account of its fishery.

With the experience I acquired during such voyages, I became one of most skilful navigators in Europe. On August 3, 1492, I set sail with a fleet of three ships—the '*Nina*', the '*Pinta*' and the '*Santa Maria*'—from Palos, on River Tinto in southern Spain and reached the East Indies. In command of six ships, three with explorers and three with provisions, I set sail westward, on May 30, 1498. The first land sighting was at Trinidad, which was named in honour of the **Holy Trinity**.

I was of the opinion, from the statements of several ancient writers, that India was a country of immense size, extending far to the east and that it might be most easily reached by sailing westward around the spherical globe. I was the first European to sail across the Atlantic Ocean and successfully land on the American continent. I died on May 20, 1506.

Christopher Columbus

The United States celebrates a national holiday in honour of Columbus (on the Monday closest to October 12). Though apparently uncultivated, the landmass of America, when Columbus landed on it, was populous. Inhabitants were seen coming out from all parts of the woods and running to the shore. They were perfectly naked and stood gazing at the ships.

I was born on August 4, 1929 in Khandwa. I was the youngest in the family. My father, Kunjhalal Ganguly, was a lawyer. My mother Gauri Devi was from a wealthy family and had received an education denied in those days to most girls. I had two brothers and a sister. Both my brothers were famous film stars. As a young boy, I was full of mischief and pranks. I loved to play and almost never tired of seeking amusements.

I used to sing for my parents and they would give me money as a small token. Moving to Bombay to try out a singing career in films, I was rejected a number of times. On my brother's advice, I tried out acting. It was during a small role in the movie *Ziddi* that Khemchand Prakash heard me sing and became impressed. He gave a song to sing: '*Marne ki duayen kyon maangon. . . .*' My uninhibited antics and spontaneity made me one of the greatest comedians of Indian cinema.

S.D. Burman was visiting my elder brother when he heard me sing in my bath. Burman advised me to develop my own style. S.D. Burman took me up, and what followed was a musical hit in *Aradhana* with '*Mere sapnon ki rani*'. I was initially taken quite lightly as a singer and was given mainly lighter songs by Burman. But with '*Dukhi man mere*' in *Funtoosh* (1956), I began to be taken seriously as a singer.

By now I was also a major star acting opposite the top heroines of the day. I sang for myself and gave playback only for Dev Anand. I reached the peak as an actor with *Chalti ka Naam Gaadi* (1958) which starred all the three Ganguly brothers. After my marriage to Ruma Devi disintegrated, I married Madhubala. *Door Gagan ki Chaon Main* (1964) confirmed my acting talent in a serious film.

Kishore Kumar

As Kishore's fame grew, so did his eccentricities. He put up a board outside his house saying 'THIS IS A LUNATIC ASYLUM'. He reportedly spoke to his trees in his backyard, addressing each by a special name. After Madhubala, he married Yogita Bali; this marriage lasted about a month. He then married his fourth wife Leena Chandavarkar. He died due to a massive heart attack in 1987.

I was born in Boston, Massachusetts, on January 17, 1706, as the 10th son of a soap-maker, Josiah. My mother was Abiah Folger, the second wife of my father. In all, my father had 17 children. I loved to read and as a young child of about 12 years, I was apprenticed to my brother, James, who was a printer. After helping James compose pamphlets and set type, I would sell our products in the streets. When I was 15, my brother started *The New England Courant*, the first newspaper in Boston.

I was not allowed to write for it, so I began writing letters under a **pseudonym**, Silence Dogood. They were a smash hit. I left home when I was 17 and became an apprentice printer in Philadelphia. Wishing to set up my own print shop, I went to London to buy fonts and printing equipment with the word of the Governor that he would fund me. Though the Governor did not keep his word, I was able to return home and open my shop.

In 1729, I bought the newspaper, *Pennsylvania Gazette.* My newspaper soon became the most successful and influential one. This newspaper printed the first political cartoon, done by me. In 1731, I founded the first public library in America. In 1732, I began publishing *Poor Richard's Almanac*, an annual collection of stories and insights about life, love, politics and other human activities. I helped launch projects to develop Philadelphia's streets.

In 1736, I organised Philadelphia's Union Fire Company, the first in the city. My famous saying, "An ounce of prevention is worth a pound of cure," is actually advice that I gave for fire fighting. In 1743, I invented a heat-efficient stove. In 1747, I began experiments to prove that light was an electrical phenomenon. I ended up inventing the lighting rod. My experiments with kite flying, with a key attached to the string, on stormy nights is famous.

Benjamin Franklin

Franklin served as a clerk, and later as assembly man in the Pennsylvania General Assembly from 1736 to 1757. In 1762, he was again elected to the Assembly. He organised the postal system, became Postmaster General and helped Thomas Jefferson to write the Declaration of Independence, signed on July 4, 1776. His inventions include swim fins and bifocals. He died on April 17, 1790, and was mourned across the world.

I was born on February 11, 1847 in Milan, Ohio. When I was seven-years old, my family moved to Michigan, and my father to the Fort Gratiot military post as a carpenter. I entered school but my teachers considered me a dull student. I couldn't hear properly and so couldn't follow much of what was being taught at school. My school attendance grew irregular and at the same time, I became a voracious reader.

When I was 10, I set up a laboratory in our basement. My mother went along with it for a while, but when she could not stand the smell of chemicals any more, she made it clear to me to leave it all; so I became a trainboy on the Grand Trunk Railway. An empty freight car became my new laboratory. My first invention was an automatic telegraph repeater. My first patent was for an electric vote recorder.

My favourite invention was the phonograph, patented in 1877. In 1883, I discovered that electrons flowed from incandescent filaments. In 1885, I patented a method to transmit telegraphic signals over short distances. When I was born, homes were lit with lamps and candles. By the time I died, cities were lit up by electricity. In my honour, electric lights in USA were dimmed for one minute on October 21, 1931, a few days after my death.

I patented the first fluorescent lamp in 1896. Among my other inventions were the universal motor, which used alternating or direct current, the motion picture camera, and the electric safety lantern for miners. To reduce costs, I asked my father to help me build a new laboratory in Menlo Park, New Jersey. I came to be known as the 'Wizard of Menlo Park'. I believed that "genius is one per cent inspiration and 99 per cent perspiration."

Thomas Alva Edison

While working for the railroad, Thomas Alva Edison saved the life of a station official's child, who had fallen onto the tracks of an oncoming train. For his bravery, the boy's father taught Edison how to use the telegraph. This changed Edison's life. In 1889, he consolidated his many companies into the Edison General Electric Company, known today as GE. He died on October 18, 1931.

I am an Emperor of India, born at Umarkot, Sind in 1542. I inherited the throne at the age of 13, in 1556, after the sudden death of my father. I went through bouts of depression and also had epileptic fits early in life. I ruled for almost half a century. In the early years of my rule, I was supported by Bairam Khan, who faithfully helped me govern my huge empire.

The early years of my reign saw civil war and rebellion. After I had put down all revolts against my kingdom and triumphed over my enemies within the empire, I turned to foreign conquest, extending my control to the whole of northern India. I reformed the tax system, promoted commerce, encouraged science, literature, and the arts, and abolished slavery.

My religious tolerance strengthened the empire. In 1579 I abolished the *jaziya*, a tax imposed on non-Muslims. I defeated an almost impregnable fortress in Rajasthan and went on to marry the Rajput princess, Jodhabai, whom I permitted to conduct Hindu rites after marriage. I built a capital, **Fatehpur Sikri**, around the tomb of a Sufi saint who had foretold the birth of my son. I invited priests of various religions, including Portuguese Jesuits from Goa, to debate on all the faiths in my court.

Though I myself was an illiterate man, I loved learning and disputation. I am said to have suffered from **dyslexia**, which was why I could never learn how to read and write. My administrative and economic reforms formed the basis of my empire for a century after I died. Birbal, Abul Fazl and Tansen were known as jewels of my court. I had nine such jewels. The first great Mughal monument, Humayun's tomb, was erected during my reign in the 1560s.

Akbar

Akbar's full name was Jalal-ud-Din Muhammad Akbar. He died in 1605. His descendants, most notably his great-grandson, Aurangzeb overturned the religious tolerance established by Akbar for Mughal rule. Aurangzeb plundered and destroyed Hindu temples and revived the *jaziya* system of taxation.

I was born on December 26, 1893 in Hunan. I lived in a village till I was 17, when I went to a school in Changsha, the capital of Hunan. That same year, a revolution led by Dr Sun Yat-Sen overthrew the imperial government and I left my studies. After spending some time with the revolutionary army, I studied on my own and familiarised myself with the works of Darwin, Mill and Rousseau. As I needed money, I joined a teaching course. I began to enjoy Chinese literature.

Instead of becoming a teacher, I went to Peking as an assistant in the university library. The library chief, Li Ta-chao, and a professor of literature, Chen Tu-hsui, who were radical Marxists, became my friends. We founded the Chinese Communist Party, the CCP in 1921, after thousands of students in 1919 protested against the concessions given to Japan under the Paris Peace Conference. I edited radical magazines, organised trade unions, and became the CCP's General Secretary.

By 1925, the CCP still had only 900 members, and I joined Sun Yat-Sen's Nationalist Party, the Kuomintang. After Sun Yat-Sen died, a young General, Chiang Kai-Shek, took control and by 1927, almost half of China was under the control of **Kuomintang**. Some powerful Kuomintang officials were landlords and I thus did not have the support of either the Kuomintang or of Stalin. I preferred a peasant uprising rather than that of the workers.

Chiang too saw the rise of the CCP and ordered the massacre of communists and militant workers in cities. In 1935, we captured Tsunyi, and I was elected Chairman of the Chinese Communist Party. In our first years, over three million people were killed for voicing their minds. Dissenters were taken as prisoners, executed or subjugated to terrible brainwashing sessions.

Mao Tse Tung

In 1976, Mao died of **Parkinson's disease**. While he shared power with Chou En-lai, Lin Piao and Liu Shao-chi, he was exalted among the people as an ideological example. Mao's 'greatest reform in history' was the Agrarian Reform Law which destroyed the landlord class, and the land was distributed to the peasants. Manufacturing, mining, transport and communications were emphasised upon.

I was born on January 17, 1942, in Louisville, Kentucky. My father was a signboard and mural painter, and my mother worked as a domestic help. When I was 12, my bicycle was stolen. I reported it to a policeman, Joe Elsby Martin, who supervised the training of young boxers and had a television show called Tomorrow's Champions. Martin arranged for me to train with Fred Stoner.

During high school, I won 100 out of 108 matches and earned six Kentucky, two National Golden Glove Championships, and two Amateur Athletic Union Championships. In the 1960 Olympics at Rome, at the age of 18, I won the gold medal in the light heavyweight category. After the Olympics, I became a professional. I fought Sonny Liston for the World Heavyweight Championship title and defeated him.

Disgusted with racism in America, I tossed my Olympic gold medal into a river after I was refused service at a soda counter because of my colour. I defeated Liston again at a rematch in June 1965, with a knockout punch to the side of his head. I was disliked by many because of my conversion to Islam. My anti-war stance on US involvement in Vietnam too did not help. In May 1967, I was stripped of my title and my boxing licence was cancelled by the World Boxing Association.

My first fight after this was against Jerry Quarry in 1970 at Atlanta. I won by knocking out Quarry in the third round. After I recovered my licence, I fought Joe Frazier, the reigning heavyweight champion, in 1971. I lost this fight; my first defeat as a professional. In 1975, while fighting Frazier for the third time, I won. On June 26, 1979, at the age of 37, I retired as champion with a professional record of 59 victories and three defeats.

Cassius Clay Jr., alias Muhammed Ali

In 1980, Ali returned to fight Larry Holmes. Holmes was declared winner with a technical knockout. A year later, Ali boxed professionally for the last time, against Trevor Berbick. At the 1996 Olympic Games in Atlanta, he was honoured by being asked to light the torch during the opening ceremony. In 1999, Ali became the first boxer to appear on a **Wheaties box**.

I was born in a Sikh family of farmers in the village of Banga of Layalpur district of Punjab (now in Pakistan) on September 27, 1907. My family stood for patriotism, reform, and freedom of the country. My grandfather was drawn to **Arya Samaj**, a reformist movement of Hinduism, while my father and uncle were jailed for alleged anti-British activities. I was brought up in a politically charged state of Punjab which was left with a seething memory of the **Jallianwala Bagh** massacre.

As a lad of 14, I went to this spot and collected soil in my lunch box as a memento for life. To avoid early marriage, I ran away from home and became a member of the youth organisation, Noujawan Bharat Sabha, which had membership of all sects and religions. I met Chandra Shekhar Sharma (Azad), B.K. Dutt and other revolutionaries. They used to print handouts and newspapers in secret and spread political awareness in India.

In Lahore, Lala Lajpat Rai and Pandit Madan Mohan Malaviya decided to protest against the British about their displeasure. It was a silent protest march, yet the police chief, Scott, had banned meetings or processions. Thousands joined, without giving room for any untoward incident. Even then, Scott beat Lala Lajpat Rai who succumbed to the injuries. I was an eye witness and and with the help of Azad, Rajguru and Sukhdev plotted to kill Scott.

Under the Defence of India Act, British gave more power to the police to arrest persons and to stop processions with suspicious movements and actions. I, who was in hiding all this while, volunteered to throw a bomb in the central assembly where the meeting to pass an ordinance was being held. I was caught and put in prison. I wanted to be shot like a soldier, but, my plea was rejected, and I was hanged on March 23, 1931.

Bhagat Singh

Bhagat Singh became a legendary hero for the masses. Innumerable songs were composed about him, and the youth throughout the country made him their ideal. He became a symbol of bravery and a goal to free India from the British yoke.

I was born as Manikarnika, on 19th November 1835 in Varanasi. I belonged to a wealthy, high caste family. After I lost my mother at the age of four, my father completed my education. Along with my adopted brothers I was given martial training, such as horse riding, fencing and shooting. I got married to Raja Gangadhar Rao, the Maharaja of Jhansi in 1842.

In 1851, I gave birth to a son who died when he was just four-months old. After this tragedy I adopted Damodar Rao as my son. Maharaja Gangadhar Rao expired on 21 November 1853, when I was 18-years old. Although I was so young I did not lose my sense of courage and responsibility. Under the Doctrine of Lapse, Lord Dalhousie, the Governor General of British India, rejected Damodar Rao as the legal heir and decided to annex the state of Jhansi.

In March 1854, the British offered me an annual pension of Rs 60,000 and in return ordered me to leave Jhansi. I was determined not to give up my Jhansi. I persevered to strengthen the defence of Jhansi with a volunteer army of 14,000 patriots. I also recruited women and gave them military training. I was known for my generosity towards my subordinates. Jhansi was attacked by the British in 1858. There was fierce shelling of Jhansi. There were four days of fire, pillage, murder and looting without distinction.

With my son strapped tightly to my back, I fought valiantly, using the sword with both my hands. When the situation went out of control, I escaped with some of my warriors over a hundred miles away to Kalpi. At Kalpi I was joined by other patriots like Tatia Tope. On June 1, 1885, we were successful in our attempt to capture the fortress city. Three weeks later, on 18th June, at the age of 22 years, I lost my life when I came under British assault. I was then cremated by my faithful servants.

Rani Lakshmi Bai

Known as Rani Lakshmi Bai, she was a significant symbol of resistance and threat against the British Raj. They were in awe of her brave patriotism and martyrdom. The Indian National Army named its first female unit after her.

I was born in Birmington, Alabama, USA. My parents were track coaches and I had three brothers and sisters. I was considered the least impressive athlete in the family. Though I qualified for the 1980 Olympics, but because of a boycott of the Moscow Games by the USA, I could not participate. The 1983 World Championship in Helsinki was my first international competition. I won three gold medals for 100 m, long jump and the 4×100 m relay.

In the 1984 Olympics, I won four well-deserved medals for 100 m, 200 m, 4×100 m relays and long jump. I won two golds in the 1988 Olympics for 100 m and long jump. I received the third consecutive gold medal in long jump in the 1992 Olympics. I did lose in the long jump competition for a decade, but went on to win 65 consecutive competitions.

When, at the age of 35, I won my fourth consecutive Olympic long jump medal in 1996, *The Sports Illustrated*'s Rick Reilly wrote about me: "You try to give a man a gold watch, and he steals your gold medal instead. You ask him to pass the torch, he sets your Olympics on fire." With my 1996 gold medal, I received the maximum number of Olympic golds along with swimmer Mark Spitz, long-distance runner Paavo Nurmi and gymnast Larysa Latynina.

I was the third track-and-field athlete to win four gold medals in a row in one Olympics, after Americans Al Kraenzlein and Jesse Owens. The gold medal for the 100 m dash in the 1988 Olympics was given to me after Ben Johnson was disqualified for drug abuse. In the 1996 Atlanta Games, I won the gold, leaving behind the first runner-up, James Beckford. I won 10 Olympic medals comprising nine golds and one silver.

Carl Lewis

When Carl's father died of cancer, Carl put his gold medal won at the 100 m race in Los Angeles in the coffin. He then looked at his mother and said: "Don't worry, I'll win another one!" He was never known for humility. He was proud and wasn't ashamed to show it.

My father was Viswanath Datta and my mother was Bhuvaneshwari Devi. I was born on January 12, 1863 in Calcutta. As a child I was very lively and naughty but my mother knew how to control me. She would immediately pour a few pots of water on my head, saying all the while, "Shiva, Shiva, Shiva!". This would immediately quieten me and I would start meditating.

I accepted the philosophies of the western mind along with science. At the same time, I was very keen to learn about God. I questioned people who were said to be holy, asking them if they had seen God. As a child too, I was always fascinated by the *sanyasis* and would give anything that was at hand to them as alms. Even before I was six, I knew all the stories in ***Ramayana*** and ***Mahabharata*** by heart.

I found my guru in Sri Ramakrishna, who allayed my doubts, gave me vision of God, and transformed me into a sage and prophet with the authority to teach. After Sri Ramakrishna's death, I renounced the world and travelled across the country. Accepting an opportunity to represent Hinduism at Chicago's Parliament of Religions in 1893, I was recognised and admired in America.

There was a ready forum for my spiritual teachings. I returned to India and founded the Ramakrishna Math and Mission. I travelled throughout the country. I had spread ***Vedanta*** philosophy and religion in America and England. I awakened India to a new national consciousness. I died on July 4, 1902, after a second, much shorter journey to the West. My lectures and writings have been compiled and published in nine volumes.

Swami Vivekananda

On July 4, 1902, Swami Vivekananda sat down to meditate in his room at Belur Math. And when some of the monks went to see him, he had already passed away. He was 39-years old. Today, the Ramakrishna Mission has over 138 permanent centres in India and 33 centres abroad.

I was born in 1870, in Ulyanovsk, Russia, and studied at Kazan and St. Petersburg. My name at birth was Vladimir Ilyich Ulyanovand. I graduated in law. I became involved in the revolution early in life, especially after my brother was stopped from completing his law studies for indulging in revolutionary activities. I soon renounced my legal practice and concentrated on learning and propagating the works of Karl Marx. I was exiled to Siberia in 1895.

I caused the Bolshevik and Menshevik factions of the Russian Social Democratic Labour Party to split. The Bolsheviks were headed by me. There was competition for supremacy with Plekhanov, Kautsky, and other Marxists. With the outbreak of revolution in 1905, I returned to Russia. I left Russia in 1907 and after that mainly engaged myself in theoretical debates and thoughts.

In October 1917, I led the **Bolshevik revolution** and became head of the first Soviet government. The first thing I did was to propose an armistice with Germany and abolish private ownership of land and distribute it among the peasants. Banks were nationalised, a council was established to revive the economy, and workers were given control over factory production. Atheism became the official 'religion'.

My New Economic Policy in 1921, which allowed some privatisation was seen by some as a compromise with capitalism. I became chairman of the Council of People's Commissars with Trotsky, Stalin, and Rykov as the other chief members. I now became more or less a dictator. All opposition was ruthlessly suppressed by the Cheka, or my political police. I suffered a stroke in 1922 and a subsequent stroke deprived me of speech.

Vladimir Ilyich Lenin

After Lenin's death, Stalin became the leader, which was something Lenin did not recommend. Lenin's body was embalmed and placed in a mausoleum in Red Square. In 1924, Petrograd was renamed Leningrad in his honour, but since the collapse of communism, the city has once more returned to the name of St. Petersburg.

I was born on June 26, 1892, in Hillsboro, West Virginia, to missionaries Absalom and Caroline Sydenstricker, who were missionaries stationed in China. I spent almost the entire first half of my life in China. As a young girl, I absorbed the language and culture of my adopted land. I grew up with '**mentally bifocal**', and was able to appreciate and love two very different cultures, each on its own terms.

After graduating in 1914 from Randolph-Macon Women's College in Lynchburg, Virginia, I returned to China and taught Chinese boys at a missionary school until 1917, when I married an American agriculturalist. After a complicated pregnancy, in 1921, I gave birth to a daughter, Carol. My daughter was retarded. In January 1930, I started writing my *Wang Lung* novel, an epic tale of a Chinese peasant's relationship with his family and the land that sustained them.

I started taking interest in the problems of retarded and handicapped children after my own experiences with my daughter. For the first time, I wrote about Carol, initially as an article in *Ladies' Home Journal* and later in book form, *The Child who Never Grew.* Parents of retarded children overwhelmed me with letters of relief on knowing that they were not alone in their struggle.

Upon the publication of my epic novel in 1931, *Good Earth* became a bestseller and stayed a bestseller longer than any book before. In 1932, it received the Pulitzer Prize for literature. I now permanantly moved to USA. By 1940, I was one of the most popular and widely translated authors in the world. I got the 1938 Nobel Prize for literature.

Pearl S. Buck

Pearl died on March 6, 1973, and was buried in the grounds of her Pennsylvania farmhouse, now the headquarters of the Pearl S. Buck Foundation. She launched the Welcome House to find adoptive homes for American-born bi-racial children. This expanded to dozens of homes for mixed-race children. The Pearl S. Buck Foundation clothes, feeds, educates, and provides employment to often-abandoned children.

I was born on August 12, 1919 at Ahmedabad. My early education was at a private school run by my parents. After passing inter-science from Gujarat College in Ahmedabad, I joined St. John's College, Cambridge (UK) where I took my **Tripos** in natural sciences in 1939. The outbreak of Second World War necessitated my return to India where I took up cosmic-ray research under the guidance of Nobel laureate, Sir C.V. Raman, at the Indian Institute of Science in Bangalore.

In 1947, I was awarded a doctorate by Cambridge University for my thesis, 'Cosmic Ray Investigations in Tropical Latitudes'. On return to India, I founded the Physical Research Laboratory (PRL) in November 1947 at Ahmedabad where I continued my scientific activities. In 1947, I founded Ahmedabad Textile Industries' Research Association (ATIRA) which I directed until 1956. Between 1950 and 1966, I was instrumental in establishing a chain of industries in Baroda.

Realising the need for professional management education in India, I founded the Indian Institute of Management (IIM) in 1962 and directed it until 1965. In 1962, I took over the responsibility of organising space research in India as Chairman of Indian National Committee for Space Research (INCOSPAR). With active support from Homi Bhabha (1906-1966), I set up the first rocket launching station (TERLS) in the country at Thumba, near Thiruvananthapuram.

I was appointed Chairman of the Atomic Energy Commission. I received many awards: Bhatnagar Medal (1962), Padma Bhushan (1966), president of the physics section of the Indian Science Congress (1962), president of the General Conference of the IAEA (1970), vice-president, Fourth UN Conference on 'Peaceful Uses of Atomic Energy' (1971).

Vikram Sarabhai

Vikram Sarabhai was awarded the Shanti Swaroop Bhatnagar Award for physics in 1962 and was honoured with Padma Bhushan in 1966. Padma Vibhushan was awarded to him posthumously. Sarabhai passed away in his sleep on December 31, 1971. He was truly a rare combination of an innovator, industrialist and visionary.

I was born on July 30, 1863 in Dearborn, Michigan, into a farming family. As a young man, I became an excellent self-taught mechanic and machinist. At the age of 16, I left the farm and went to Detroit, as an apprentice at a machine shop. Months later I began to work with steam engines at the Detroit Dry Dock Company, where I saw the internal combustion engine for the first time. At 28, I joined Thomas Edison's Detroit Illuminating Company, where I became the chief engineer.

In my spare time I began to build my first car, the quadricycle. In June 1896, I took my first ride in my first automobile. The quadricycle, however, broke down. In 1899, I created a better looking motorcar with the help of wealthy businessman, William Murphy. In the same year I founded the Detroit Automobile Company and within three years I built an improved, more reliable quadricycle, using a four-cylinder, 36-horsepower racing engine.

In 1901, my car beat what was then the world's fastest automobile in a race before a crowd of 8,000 people in Grosse Pointe, Michigan. In 1903, I started my own car company, and by January 1904, I sold 658 vehicles. By 1908, I built the famous Model T, a car that was affordable even for the middle class. As many as 720,000 Model Ts were sold by 1916.

I was one of the first to introduce time-clocks to monitor the exact minute a worker arrived at his job, took his lunch, and left his job. I was the first to begin the concept of mass production of cars. Most people in USA were shocked when they read about my anti-Semitism, which I published weekly for two years in unsigned articles in my own newspaper, *The Dearborn Independent.* Adolf Hitler had my framed picture on his wall. I am the only US citizen mentioned in his *Mein Kampf.*

Henry Ford

Henry Ford was an active philanthropist throughout his life. He built a hospital for his employees in Detroit, and in 1936 established the Ford Foundation for the purpose of "advancing human welfare". Since its founding, the Ford Foundation has issued more than $8 billion in grants worldwide. Ford died at his estate, in Dearborn, Michigan in 1947, at the age of 84.

I was born on December 27, 1822 in the small town of Dole, as the son of a tanner. I studied in the College of Arbois and at Besancon, from where I graduated in arts in 1840. I stood at third place in the prestigious ***Ecole Normale Superieure*** of Paris, and for my doctorate, I pursued **crystallography**, a science that was quite unknown then. I researched on optical properties of crystals of the salts of tartrates and paratartrates.

At 26, the French government made me a member of the Legion of Honour, and Britain's Royal Society presented me with the Copley Medal. At 31, I became professor of chemistry and Dean of Sciences at the new University of Lille. I discovered that contamination was caused by living organisms, which were destroyed by heating. I also connected the phenomenon of fermentation or putrefaction to this contamination, which helped preserve wine, beer, and milk.

After my father and two daughters died by typhoid fever, I suffered a cerebral haemorrhage. During the Franco-Prussian War, I saw the numerous wounded and this encouraged me to talk on my microbial theory of disease and infection to the military medical corps. They finally agreed to the sterilisation of instruments and the steaming of bandages. This saw a drastic drop in infections and deaths. In 1873, I was made a member of the French Academy of Medicine without a medical degree.

After a serious outbreak of anthrax, I inoculated the sick animals with anthrax bacilli and succeeded in immunising them. My ultimate triumph was the control of rabies, in 1884. **Rabies** is seen mostly in dogs, and a bite by such a dog causes hydrophobia in humans. I first saved the life of a 12-year-old boy, Joseph Meister. In 1888, France founded the Pasteur Institute, one of the most productive centres of biological study in the world today.

Louis Pasteur

On September 28, 1895, Pasteur died near Saint-Cloud in Paris. His last words were: "One must work; one must work. I have done what I could." He was buried in a crypt in the Pasteur Institute. In 1940, Germans came again to Paris and a German officer wanted to see the tomb of Pasteur. The old French guard there refused to open the gate. When the German insisted, he killed himself. He was Joseph Meister, the boy Pasteur had saved long ago.

I was a poet and philosopher, born in 1861, in Calcutta. I was the youngest son of Debendranath Tagore, a leader of the **Brahmo Samaj**. I was educated at home. I was sent to England for formal schooling at the age of 17, but did not finish my studies there. When I was older, apart from everything else, I managed the family estates, which increased my interest in social reform. I also started an experimental school for education. I started to compose poems at the age of eight.

My collection of poems appeared when I was 17; it was published by my friend who wanted to surprise me. My early education came from tutors and then a variety of schools, among them the Bengal Academy, where I studied history and culture. At University College, London, I studied law but left after a year, as I did not like the weather. In 1883, I married Mrinalini Devi Raichaudhuri, with whom I had two sons and three daughters.

In 1890, I moved to East Bengal where I wrote seven volumes of poetry including *Sonar Tari* (*The Golden Boat*) in 1894 and *Khanika* in 1900. In England I started to compose the poem *Bhanga Hriday* (*A Broken Heart*). I was the first Indian to bring an element of philosophical realism to my novels. Among my early major prose works are *Choker Bali* (1903, *Eyesore*) and *Nashtanir* (1901, *The Broken Nest*) published first serially.

My wife died in 1902, next year my daughter died and in 1907, I lost my younger son. I am best known for my poetic works, notably *Gitanjali* (1912, *Song Offering*) and short stories, such as *Galpaguccha* (1912, *A Bunch of Stories*). I wrote my most important works in Bengali, but I often translated my poems into English. At the age of 70, I took up painting. I was also a composer, setting hundreds of poems to music.

Rabindranath Tagore

In 1901, Tagore founded the **Vishwa Bharati**, to teach Western and Indian philosophy and education. He received the Nobel Prize for literature in 1913, the first Asian to do so. He was knighted in 1915, an honour which he returned in 1919 as a protest against British policy. 'Our Golden Bengal' became the national anthem of Bangladesh. Only hours before he died on August 7, 1941, he dedicated his last poem to the nation.

I was born on April 20, 1889 at Braunau in Austria on River Inn. My father was an Austrian customs official. I was very impressed by the successes of the anti-Semitic, nationalist Christian Socialist Party of Vienna mayor, Karl Lueger. Under Lueger's influence, I first developed my fanatical anti-Semitism and racial theories. I was influenced by the pseudo-scientific and neo-religious writings of the race ideologist and anti-Semite, Lanz von Liebenfels.

During the First World War, I fought on Germany's western front with distinction but did not get any promotion beyond the rank of corporal. I was injured twice and won several awards for bravery, along with the Iron Cross, First Class. In April 1921, I became Fuhrer or head of the renamed National Socialist German Workers' Party (NSDAP), the official name of the Nazi Party. I was tried for treason and given a year's imprisonment in the old fort of Landsberg for staging the Nazi Beer Hall Putsch in 1923.

During my prison term, I described my major plans and beliefs to my close friend, Rudolf Hess. On January 30, 1933, I was asked to head a coalition government of Nazis, conservative German nationalists, and several prominent independents. In March 1935 I repudiated the Treaty of Versailles by reintroducing conscription in Germany. I set about building a massive military machine, including a new Navy (the Kriegsmarine) and an Air Force (the Luftwaffe).

In July 1936, during the Spanish Civil War, I supported General Francisco Franco, to rebel against the elected Popular Front government of Spain. Spain served as a testing ground for Germany's new armed forces and their methods, including the bombing of undefended towns such as Guernica, which was destroyed by the Luftwaffe in April 1937. On September 1, 1939, I initiated the Second World War with the invasion of Poland. I immediately followed this with the massacre of Jews.

Adolf Hitler

In the last days of the Third Reich, Hitler entered into his underground bunker in Berlin. He ordered Germany to be destroyed, expelled his trusted lieutenants, Himmler and Goring, and made a last, theatrical appeal. He committed suicide on April 30, 1945, leaving the country's administration in the hands of non-Nazi, Karl Doenitz.

I was born on August 15, 1769, in the city of Ajaccio, in the Corsican Island. I was the fourth of 11 children of my parents. My mother, Letizia, was a hard, austere woman, toughened by war, who punished her children to teach them sacrifice and discipline. After elementary education in Ajaccio, I was sent in January 1779 to the College of Autun in the Duchy of Burgundy. In May 1779, I was transferred to the more fashionable College of Brienne, another military college.

In October 1784, I earned an appointment to the **École Militaire** of Paris. The siege of Toulon provided me the first opportunity to display my ability as an artillery officer and I was promoted to the rank of Brigadier General. On June 10, 1793, I set sail for France with my widowed mother and siblings, carrying all that we had owned in the world. In 1795, I met Josephine de Beauharnais, and married her on March 9, 1796. Josephine and I were crowned Empress and Emperor in 1804.

By 1802, I became the most popular dictator France had ever known, and I was given the position of First Consul for life, with the right to name my successor. I led armies all over Europe and conquered all, except England. Joseph Fouche, head of the secret police, helped me reach every aspect of French society through a vast network of spies. Some of the campaigns and wars I led were against Egypt, Prussia, Russia, Austria and Italy.

My small stature earned me the nickname of the 'Little Corporal'. I was finally defeated at the **Battle of Waterloo** by combined British and Prussian armies under the Duke of Wellington and Gebhard von Blücher on June 18, 1815. I was sent into exile on the island of St. Helena, where I died on May 5, 1821. On the island, I was guarded by 2,000 soldiers, and two ships circled the island 24 hours a day. My house was a wooden bungalow that had once been a row of cattle stalls.

Napoleon Bonaparte

"To die is nothing," Napoleon said, "but to live defeated and without glory is to die every day." Day after day, he dictated his memoirs, forging the story of his life into the stuff of legend. He was always with his soldiers and fought along with them as the bravest amongst them. Josephine and Napoleon's romance is famous with his love letters being perhaps the best written.

I was born in Nadiad in present-day Gujarat, in 1875. I completed my schooling and in the thirties, went to Britain to qualify as a barrister. I returned to India around the same time as Gandhi returned to India from South Africa, on the eve of the First World War, and we met shortly thereafter. I joined Gandhi in representing the weavers in the dispute with millowners in Ahmedabad in 1918, and played a pivotal role in helping to redress the grievances of peasants in Kheda district.

I studied law in England but returned (1915) to India and practised in Ahmedabad. Influenced by the nationalist leader Mohandas Gandhi, I joined the civil disobedience movement and successfully organised (1928) the landowners of Bardoli against British tax increases. In 1931, I served as president of the Indian National Congress. The British imprisoned me a number of times for my activities.

I used to earn thousands of rupees every month as a lawyer. But I gave up my lucrative practice in order to fight for the freedom of the country. As a leader of the farmers, I forced the mighty British government to accept defeat. I was sent to prison. As the Deputy Prime Minister of free India, I brought about the merger of many princely states into the Indian Union, and became the architect of the integrity of united India.

Though a staunch Hindu, I had a keen appreciation of the syncretic culture of India, and I recognised that India had furnished a hospitable home to adherents of various religions over the centuries. I contributed very substantially to the deliberations of the Constituent Assembly, and it has not always been recognised that the protection and privileges guaranteed to minorities in the Indian Constitution under Articles 29 and 30 owe much to my vigilance.

Sardar Patel

Sardar Patel is still remembered as one of the principal architects of India's Independence and in persuading rulers of states to join the Indian Union. He is also known as the 'man of steel'. His devotion to the idea of the nation-state also points to the limitations of his thinking, as he was incapable of offering the critique of modernity that Gandhi pioneered.

I was an illiterate and pious peasant girl born on January 6, around the year 1412, in the village of Domremy, in eastern France. When I was about 13-years old, I began to see religious visions and hearing the voice of saints. By the time I was 17, I could hear the saintly voices urging me persistently to go to the local commander at Vaucouleurs to take me to the Royal Court.

I finally obeyed the voices in 1428, and asked a family relative, Durand Lassois, to take me to Vaucouleurs to speak with the garrison commander, Lord Robert de Baudricour. Lord Robert helped me to meet Charles VII, the king of France. I reminded King Charles about a prayer that he had made to God the previous year, and he was convinced that I was not lying about my visions and voices. He gave me a suit of amour and some troops and sent me to Orleans, which was under attack.

In Orleans, I led a series of skilful assaults that made the British flee in about a week. Despite being a girl, I had no time for frills, hence I normally dressed in male clothes. I always kept this clothing laced on tightly, even when camping in the fields with soldiers. While trying to recapture Paris, I was taken prisoner by the Burgundians. They handed me over to the English for 16,000 francs.

Among my soldier friends, I was known as la Pucelle or the maid. After I went through what I believe was an unfair trial in Rouen, I was declared a heretic. I was burned at the stake before a huge crowd. I was declared a saint in 1920 by Pope Benedict XV. The day of my death, May 30, became my feast day. By the beginning of the 19th century, even people in England began to admit that I was really not a 'witch' as they thought.

Joan of Arc

Arrested and thrown into prison as a witch, Joan of Arc was not allowed a counsel, and was confined to a prison guarded by English soldiers. She was initially kept in an iron cage, chained by the neck, hands, and feet. She was not allowed to attend church. When she came in front of the judges, her simplicity, piety, and common sense appeared at every turn, despite the attempts of the judges to confuse her. She acquired fame for her indomitable spirit.

I was born on January 15, 1929, at the family home, in Atlanta, Georgia. My father was a minister of the church. I was the first son and second child born to my parents. My first school was Yonge Street Elementary School. Because of my high score in the college entrance examination in the junior year of the high school, I advanced to Morehouse College, skipping both the 9th and 12th grades at the age of 15.

After my bachelor's degree in sociology, I attended Crozer, Theological Seminary in Chester and the University of Pennsylvania. I won the Pearl Plafker Award as an outstanding student of the graduating class, and the J. Lewis Crozer Fellowship for graduate study. In 1951, I began doctoral studies on Systematic Theology at Boston University. I also studied at Harvard University. My dissertation, *A Comparison of God in the Thinking of Paul Tillich and Henry Wieman*, was completed in 1955.

In Boston I met my future wife, Coretta Scott, who was studying at the New England Conservatory of Music. I entered the Christian *ministry* and was ordained in February 1948 at the age of 19 at Ebenezer Baptist Church, Atlanta. I decided to live and fight for the rights of Black people. In 1963, I became *Time* magazine's Man of the Year. In 1964, I was awarded the Nobel Peace Prize, becoming the youngest recipient of that prize in history.

While in Morehouse College, I attended a lecture by Modecai Johnson, president of Howard University, on Mahatma Gandhi. Johnson's lecture provided the direction I needed in life. I was assassinated on April 4, 1968, on the balcony outside the Memphis motel room, by James Earl Ray. My most famous quote is: "If a man hasn't found something he will die for, he isn't fit to live."

Dr Martin Luther King Jr.

Dr King was a pivotal figure in the civil rights movement. He was elected president of the Montgomery Improvement Association, the organisation that was responsible for the successful Montgomery Bus Boycott from 1955 to 1956. He was arrested 30 times for his participation in civil rights activities.

Born on June 9, 1949 to parents who didn't cling to the old ways, I had good education and eventually received my Ph.D. My interest in sports helped me win many titles including the Junior National Lawn Tennis Championship in 1966, the Asian Lawn Tennis Championship in 1972, and the All-India Inter-State Women's Lawn Tennis Championship in 1976.

I also won three gold as well as two silver medals at the Women's Festival of Sports held in 1976 in Delhi. I had a distinguished career in India, where I was the first female officer ever to join the Indian Police Service in July 1972. I held the position of Special Commissioner (Intelligence) with the Delhi Police prior to my UN appointment. I hold a law degree, a master's degree in political science and a Ph.D. in the field of drug abuse and domestic violence.

I am the author of the 3-C model of prison reforms consisting of literacy programme, drug abuse and mental health treatment. As Inspector General of the largest prison in any liberal democracy, the Tihar prison, I supervised 11,000 people. My eventful life has already been chronicled in my biography, *I Dare. It's Always Possible*, the first book written by me, shifts focus to the now-famous Tihar experiment.

I received the Police Medal for Gallantry as well as the Asia Region Award for Work in Prevention of Drug Abuse. In 1994, I was awarded the Ramon Magsaysay Award. In 1997, I was the recipient of the Swiss-German Joseph Beuys Award for Holistic and Innovative Management. In January 2003, Secretary-General Kofi Annan appointed me as the Civilian Police Adviser in the UN Department of Peace-keeping Operations, and I took over from Antero Lopes of Portugal.

Kiran Bedi

Kiran Bedi has many firsts to her credit—first woman IPS officer in India; first woman head of Tihar jail, the largest prison in Asia-Pacific; first person to introduce *vipasana* meditation inside Tihar and turn the conventional attitude towards crime on its head.

I was born on September 12, 1913, in Danville, Alabama. The 7th of 11 children born to Henry and Emma, I was sickly and thin, often too frail to help my older brothers and my father in the cotton fields. When I was seven, my father sold the family tools and mules, and moved to Cleveland, Ohio. I delivered groceries, loaded freight cars and worked in a shoe-repair shop. It was during this time that I discovered that I enjoyed running.

By the age of 12, I had developed into a promising sprinter. I went on to join the East Technical High School in Cleveland. Charles Riley, the track coach at Fairview Junior High, was astounded when I ran the 100-yard dash in 10 seconds flat. I set national records by running the 100-yard dash in 9.4 seconds and the 200-yard dash in 20.7 seconds. I also set a new broad jump (now called long jump) record with a leap of 24 ft, 9–5/8 ins.

I later joined the Ohio State University, where I was required to live off the campus with other African-American athletes. When I travelled with the team, I could eat at 'Blacks only' restaurants and sleep in 'Blacks only' hotels. In 1935, in the annual Big Ten Track and Field Championships, I equalled the world record for the 100-yard dash, broke the world record with a long jump of more than 26 ft, and records in 220-yard dash and in the 220-yard low hurdles.

I won a total of four gold medals at the 1936 Olympics to become the first American in the history of Olympic Track and Field to do so in a single Olympics. This was also known as the 'Hitler' Olympics. In 1970, I wrote my biography *Blackthink*, and two years later, another book, *I Have Changed*. Forty years after I had won the gold medals, I was awarded the Presidential Medal of Freedom and two years later, in 1979, the Living Legend Award.

Jesse Owens

A cigarette smoker, Jesse developed inoperable lung cancer. He died on March 31, 1980, after a long stay in Phoenix Hospital. He was buried in Chicago several days later. He was actually born and given the name James Cleveland Owens. On his first day at school, Owens gave his name as 'J. C.' and the teacher wrote it down as 'Jesse'.

I was born in Italy in 1874 to a rather wealthy Italian father and Irish mother. I was educated privately and then went to the Livorno Technical Institute. As a boy I took a keen interest in physical and electrical science and studied the works of Maxwell, Hertz, Righi, Lodge and others. I began experimenting at my family's home near Bologna. Within a year I had sent and received signals beyond the range of vision.

In 1894, I read an article on the possibility of using radio waves to communicate without wires. The most modern way to send a message then was over telegraph wires. In 1914, I was commissioned in the Italian Army as a Lieutenant. I was later promoted to Captain, and in 1916 transferred to the Navy with the rank of a Commander.

I was a member of the Italian Government's mission to the United States in 1917 and in 1919, I was appointed Italian plenipotentiary delegate to the Paris Peace Conference. I was awarded the Italian Military Medal in 1919 in recognition of my war service. In 1898, I transmitted signals across the English Channel. In 1900, I took out the famous patent No. 7777 for 'tuned or syntonic telegraphy'.

In December 1901, I used this system for transmitting the first wireless signals across the Atlantic, a distance of 2,100 miles. My first successful experiments in wireless telegraphy were made at Bologna in 1895, and in 1899, I erected a wireless station at La Spezia. I later developed short-wave radio equipment and established a worldwide radio telegraph network for the British government.

Guglielmo Marconi

Marconi got the 1909 Nobel Prize for physics, the Albert Medal of the Royal Society of Arts, the John Fritz Medal, the Kelvin Medal and the Order of St. Anne by the Tsar of Russia, among others. In 1905 he patented his horizontal directional aerial. In 1931 Marconi began research into the propagation of very short waves, opening the world's first microwave radio-telephone link between the Vatican City and the Pope's summer residence at Castel Gandolfo, in 1932.

I was forced to leave my studies in Stanford at the age of 21 to take over the family business of vegetable oils, when my father suddenly passed away in 1966. Originally called Western India Vegetable Products, the company then diversified to making *vanaspati*, later bakery fats, ethnic ingredient-based toiletries, hair care soaps, baby toiletries, lighting products and hydraulic cylinders. The shift from soaps to software was very focused. It became the No.1 listed company in the country in just 15 years.

Two years ago, I returned to Stanford, presented my dissertation and after 35 years, completed my degree in general engineering. The firm went public with the global IT services subsidiary whose gross income grew by 65 per cent to reach Rs 1,042 crore. Its technology divisions, global R&D and telecom solutions contributed 46 per cent of the software revenue, and the balance was accounted for by enterprise solutions business.

E-commerce contributed 15 per cent of enterprise solutions revenue for the year. Sales and other incomes of the Indian IT services and products business that take care of networking solutions, customer services, computers and peripherals grew by 20 per cent to Rs 825 crore. I have never sold my shares in Wipro and currently own a whopping 75 per cent of the company's shares.

I am one of the richest Indians in the world today. Despite my billions, however, I still travel economy class and stay in budget hotels. Under my leadership, a Rs 70-million company in hydrogenated cooking fats has grown to a $900-million diversified and integrated corporation. I am almost fanatical about delivering value products to customers.

Azim Hasham Premji

Azim was the prime mover behind Wipro's decision to achieve the 'Six Sigma' status. He is very clear that as a world-class organisation, what Wipro needs to be concerned about is the process, not merely the results. Wipro's code of conduct for employees is: "Don't do anything that you're unwilling to have published in tomorrow's newspaper with your photograph next to it."

I was born on August 29, 1958, in Gary, Indiana, as the 7th of nine children. I and my brothers formed a singing group when I was only five-years old. In 1968, I got an audition for Motown Records and signed a recording contract. We had 14 albums as a group and I had four solo albums. My group recorded hits such as '*I Want You Back*', '*Stop the Love You Save*', '*ABC*', and '*Dancing Machine*'. I sang the hit title song for the movie *Ben*.

In 1977, I starred in the film version of the musical hit *The Wiz*, which also featured singer Diana Ross and comic Richard Pryor. In 1979, I released the extraordinarily successful album '*Off the Wall*'; this record included the hit singles '*Rock with You*' and '*Don't Stop 'til You get Enough*' and eventually sold some 10 million copies. I got a Grammy Award for my role in the *E.T.: The Extraterrestrial* soundtrack album.

My '*Moonwalk*' and overall visual panache (combined with brilliant choreography and lavish special effects) won me an even vaster audience. I was a crucial player in the project *We are the World* which sought to combat hunger in Africa. I continued working with my brothers and our 1984 *Victory* tour was a landmark of the decade. My memoir '*Moonwalk*' was adapted into a film in 1988. I was awarded the Humanitarian of the Year trophy at the Soul Train Awards, albeit controversially, in 1993.

My album, the *Thriller*, was the best-selling album of all time and won eight Grammy Awards. In 1994, I married Lisa Marie Presley, daughter of Elvis Presley, but we divorced in 1996. I was surrounded with scandals. In February 2003, Britain's ITV network broadcast the first-ever documentary about me and I was acknowledged the world over as the controversial pop king. In 1996 I married Deborah Rowe, my dermatologist's assistant, in Australia. We were subsequently divorced.

Michael Jackson

Known as 'King of Pop', Michael Jackson was the biggest pop star of the 80s with his stunning dance moves, musical versatility and sheer star power. Even though hounded by rumours and scandals, his contribution to modern pop has been phenomenal.

I was born on August 27, 1908 at Cootamundra, New South Wales, Australia. I was the youngest with brother Victor and sisters Islet, Lilian and May. We lived in a slab hut on a property in the village of Yeo Yeo, about 25 km from Cootamundra. About three years later, my family moved to Bowral, in the Southern Highlands. I later became known as the 'Boy from Bowral'. I attended the Bowral Intermediate High School.

I played in my first cricket match at age 11 in Bowral. I scored 55 and my first century at the age of 12. I made Test debut in the 1928-29 series against England. I made 18 runs in the first innings and one in the second. I was dropped for the next Test but was picked again for the Third Test. I scored 79 in the first innings and my first Test century of 112 in the second innings. I was never again dropped from my country's team.

I won the South Australian Squash Championships in 1939, beating tennis champion Don Turnbull in five sets. At the age of 14, I left school and worked as a clerk in a Bowral Real Estate Agency. In October 1926, I played for the southern team in Country Cricket Week in Sydney. On the 1930 tour of England, I scored 334—the highest Test score at that time. I scored 452 for New South Wales against Queensland, setting a new highest first-class innings score.

The English team devised a method called '**bodyline**' to slow me down. I scored a total of 211 centuries in my career, played 52 Tests for Australia and scored 6,996 runs in Test cricket. My career Test average was 99.94, the highest ever. I ended my career in England in 1948. My autobiography is titled *Farewell to Cricket*. On March 15, 1949, I was knighted by the Governor General of Australia.

Sir Donald Bradman

As a young child, Bradman didn't have any children to play with in the neighbourhood, so he developed a ball game to play alone. He would throw a golf ball at the round brick base of a water tank, and then hit the ball with a cricket stump. This was not an easy game and without knowing it, he developed coordination and skill. The Oval, on which he played his first match at the age of 11, is now called the 'Bradman Oval'.

I was born in Shantiniketan, West Bengal, on November 3, 1933. My family is from Dhaka, Bangladesh. My ancestral home is at Wari. Old Dhaka is not far from the university campus in Ramna. My father taught chemistry at Dhaka University. My maternal grandfather taught Sanskrit and ancient and medieval Indian culture at **Shantiniketan**, where my mother and, later I, were students.

Between the age of three and six, I was at Mandalay in Burma, where my father was a visiting professor. My first school was St. Gregory's School in Dhaka from where I soon moved to Shantiniketan. I studied at Presidency College in Calcutta from 1951-53. In 1953, I went to Cambridge, to study at Trinity College, where I enrolled for B.A. (in pure economics) as I was still in my late teens. In early 1952, I had cancer of the mouth.

In 1954, I came back to India on a two-year leave, feeling that I had to complete my research on my thesis. In Calcutta, I was appointed to a Chair in economics at the newly created Jadavpur University, and was asked to set up a new Department of Economics. Since I was not yet even 23, this caused a storm of protest. I submitted my thesis that I completed in one year, rather than three, to receive the Prize Fellowship at Trinity College. I studied philosophy during that period.

In 1963, I joined the Delhi School of Economics as professor of economics. I left Delhi in 1971 to join the London School of Economics. My book, *Collective Choice and Social Welfare*, published in 1970, presents an overall view of the social choice theory. By the mid-1980s, I began to collaborate extensively with Jean Drèze, a Belgian economist. After the death of my second wife, I moved to Harvard with my children. I received the Nobel Prize in economics in 1998.

Amartya Sen

Amartya Sen has authored and co-authored more than 20 important books. Besides Delhi University, London School of Economics, Oxford University and Harvard University, he has taught as a visiting professor at MIT, Stanford, Berkeley, and Cornell. With some of the Nobel Prize money, he has set up the Pratichi Trust that will focus on education and healthcare.

I was born on October 10, 1956 in Prague, Czechoslovakia and raised in the suburb of Revnice by my mother and stepfather. My real father committed suicide when I was very young. As a lean, athletic child, I excelled in many sports, including hockey and skiing. As I grew up, my interest in tennis grew and my stepfather coached me. I brought athleticism to a new level with my training techniques, particularly cross-training. I revolutionised the game by my superb athleticism and aggressiveness.

I reached the semi-finals in the first tournament I entered, at the age of eight. At 14, I won my first national tournament, and at 16, I was the top-ranking female tennis player in Czechoslovakia. I migrated to the United States during the 1975 US Open Championship. In 1975, I reached the finals of the French Open and Australian Open, and in 1976, I lost in the semi-finals at Wimbledon to Chris Evert.

My first Grand Slam victory was a women's doubles win at Wimbledon with Chris Evert as my partner. I went on to become one of the wealthiest women in sports. I live in Aspen, Colorado, where I devote my time and money to charitable causes. Named Female Athlete of the Decade for the 1980s by the *National Sports Review*, United Press International, and the Associated Press, I was known for my athleticism and professionalism.

Mv first Wimbledon singles victory came in 1978 against Chris Evert. On July 21, 1981, I became an American citizen. I have won more singles and doubles tournaments than any other woman. My 54 total **Grand Slam** titles are second only to the legendary Margaret Smith Court, who won 62. For 10 years, Chris Evert and I battled each other for the number one world ranking, meeting 14 times in the finals of Grand Slam tournaments, and winning 10.

Martina Navratilova

Martina retired from professional singles competition in 1994 and went on to master myriad leisure sports including downhill snow skiing, snow boarding, scuba diving and competitive ice hockey. She took up photography, flying and authored several mystery novels. She is Leander Paes' mixed doubles partner, and together they have won the Wimbledon mixed doubles title.

I was born on February 16, 1959, at Wiesbaden, Germany, where my father was serving in the United States Air Force and my mother, Kay, was a surgical nurse. I was the oldest of three brothers. In 1963, my family moved to Douglaston, Queens, New York, where I was raised. At an early age, I exhibited an unusually developed eye-hand coordination and athletic ability. Although I won several junior tennis tournaments, I was never rated number one on the national junior circuit.

I attended Trinity School, a prestigious and expensive Ivy League preparatory school in Manhattan. In 1970, I was placed under Tony Palafox, a former Davis Cup player for Mexico and Harry 'Hop' Hopman, a former Australian Davis Cup coach, at the Port Washington (Long Island) Tennis Academy. A six-month suspension was imposed on me in 1975 from the Academy for a prank that I had played. I was then moved to Cove Racquet Club.

In 1977, I won the French Juniors Tournament. I became the youngest player to reach the Wimbledon semi-finals. I led Stanford University's tennis team to the NCAA Championship in 1978. After my freshman year, I decided to turn a pro. In 1978, the Association of Tennis Professionals (ATP) recognised me by conferring the Newcomer of the Year Award and ranked me number four in the world. In my first six months as a pro, I earned nearly half a million dollars.

I led the US Davis Cup team to victory over Argentina, Australia, and Italy to help the team to retain the cup. I won a total of seven Grand Slam titles in singles and seven in doubles, and was ranked number one from 1981 to 1984. In 1986, I married actress Tatum O'Neil, and retired to my home in Malibu, California. I am known for my outbursts directed at linesman, opponents, and at myself. I published my autobiography, *Serious*, in 2002.

John McEnroe

McEnroe married singer Patty Smyth in 1997 after a divorce in 1992. Currently he is a network television commentator for NBC and CBS. He devotes a lot of time to the Arthur Ashe Foundation for AIDS. McEnroe was inducted into the International Tennis Hall of Fame and named captain of the Davis Cup team. A guitar player, he plays at charity events. He has an art gallery in New York.

I was born in the beautiful city of Mysore on October 23, 1924. As a boy I pursued my love of drawing, particularly during the dull maths classes—throughout my years in Lakshmipuram primary and middle schools, and Maharajah's High School which I entered in 1937. In Mysore city, my mother allowed me, the youngest of her eight children, whose artistic talents had been recognised as early as age three by a schoolmaster, to scribble happily with chalk.

I completed the profile of my father and was going on to other things when my mother, as chirpy and mischievous as my father was stern, passed by and started laughing. Despite father's annoyance that I was "making fun of people" and defacing the floor, my mother prevailed and the drawing stayed on until my brothers and sisters could see it. "Eventually, dust, wind and time wiped off the caricature—the first in my life."

I earned my first money as a professional cartoonist during my high school years. I began by illustrating the short stories my brother R.K. Narayan wrote for *The Hindu*, receiving two rupees (about US$ 0.20) for each drawing. Soon I was able to pick up freelance work from local papers, small magazines dealing with rural development and publications for adult education.

I suffered a severe bout of typhoid in 1942, but recovered and was able to graduate from Maharaja's College of the University of Mysore. During my college years I was doing a fortnightly political cartoon for the Madras-based magazine, *Swatantra*. I joined *The Times of India* where my genial wit reached its apotheosis in the daily cartoon, 'You Said It'. Begun in 1957, it featured the bewildered and dearly beloved character, the Common Man. In September 2003, I was affected by a stroke which left me paralysed. In 2005, I was awarded the Padmashri.

R. K. Laxman

He was Laxman, India's foremost political cartoonist. He applied his special comic vision to a number of short stories, travelogues, essays and anecdotes, many of which were gathered in 1982 into a paperback volume entitled *Idle Hours*. Laxman and his wife had travelled widely in the United States, Europe and Australia.

I was born on April 16, 1889, in London. Both my parents were music hall entertainers. My mother had a nervous breakdown and my father died when I was five. My half-brother Sydney and I were admitted to Lambeth workhouse and later, to Hanwell School for Orphans and Destitute Children. We became street urchins, moving in and out of charity homes. After spending some time in an orphanage, I toured England with a children's musical troupe, the Eight Lancashire Lads.

At the age of 17, I joined the Karno music hall and toured the United States. In 1913, I was signed by the Keystone Company for a salary of $150 per week. My first film for Keystone was *Making a Living* (1914). In *Kid Auto Races at Venice* (1914), I introduced the character who became my trademark ultimately. I faced criticism in the growing atmosphere of the anti-communist crusade.

In 1952, when I was in England, I was informed that I might not be permitted back into the States because of my alleged Leftist views. I settled with my family in Switzerland. Due to public anger against me, my first European film, *A King in New York* (1957), was not released in America until 1973. In 1972, after 20 years, I was invited back to the United States to receive an honorary Academy Award.

I starred for the first time in 1915 in *The Tramp*, with Edna Purviance, who starred with me in each of my films for the next eight years. I was responsible for every aspect of my films: writing, directing, producing, casting, and editing. In 1921, I made *The Kid*, which became one of the biggest hits till date. I was awarded an honorary Academy Award in 1928 for *The Circus*. *City Lights*, a story of the tramp and a blind flower girl, was another hit.

Charlie Chaplin

Chaplin was knighted in 1975 by Queen Elizabeth II. In addition to his four wives, Chaplin was romantically linked to a number of other women, including the actresses Pola Negri and Louise Brooks. He and his last wife Oona O'Neill remained together until Chaplin's death on December 25, 1977, in Switzerland.

I was born on October 13, 1925 in the north Midlands town of Grantham, the youngest daughter of a grocer, Alfred Roberts, who greatly influenced my education and thoughts. In 1943, I just managed to enter Somerville College at Oxford but was locked in the study of chemistry. My passion was politics. My first direct experience in politics came in 1945 when I canvassed for Quentin Hogg (later Lord Halisham) in the Oxford municipal elections.

In December 1951, I married Denis Thatcher, a moderately successful owner of a paint and chemical company. In 1959, I entered Parliament at 32, representing Finchley at the high watermark postwar conservatism under Harold Macmillan. My first parliamentary position was junior minister for pensions. In 1970, I became the Education Secretary, my only cabinet post before becoming Prime Minister in 1979.

I was an abrasive leader and spent my first term removing those officials whom I deemed 'wet', overtly cautious and unwilling to accept my prescriptions for the British economy. Essentially a British nationalist, my outlook was marked by anti-communism and pro-Americanism. In a speech in January 1976, I denounced the Russians as a "failure in human and economic terms". For this, the Soviet news agency, Tass, promptly rechristened me 'Iron Lady'.

The high point of my first term occurred in 1982 when I dispatched a task force to the South Atlantic to regain control of the Falkland Islands after Argentine forces had seized them on April 1. The campaign to retake the Falklands allowed me to display my best qualities of fortitude and decisiveness. I used it to bolster domestic support at a time of widespread dissatisfaction with my economic policies.

Margaret Thatcher

In the middle of her term, Thatcher herself was viewed by many with almost visceral dislike. Thatcher announced her resignation on November 22, 1990, and was eventually replaced by one of her supporters, John Major. She became member of the House of Lords after John Major's triumph in the polls.

I was born in Raipur, a little village in Punjab, which is now a part of West Pakistan. Documents show my birth date as January 9, 1922. I was the youngest of a family of one daughter and four sons. My father was a village agricultural taxation clerk in the British Indian system of government. Although poor, my father was dedicated to educating his children.

I attended D.A.V. High School in Multan (now west Punjab), and did M.Sc. from Punjab University in Lahore. I lived in India until 1945, when a Government of India fellowship allowed me to go to England and do doctorate at the University of Liverpool. I was introduced to Western civilisation and culture. I spent a post-doctoral year (1948-1949) at the Eidgenössische Technische Hochschule in Zurich.

After a brief period in India in the fall of 1949, I returned to England where I obtained a fellowship and stayed in Cambridge from 1950 till 1952. Interest in both proteins and nucleic acids took root at that time. A job offer in 1952 from Dr Gordon M. Shrum of British Columbia took me to Vancouver. With Dr Shrum's inspiration and scientific counsel from Dr Jack Campbell, I began to work in the field of phosphate esters and nucleic acids.

I was married in 1952 to Esther Elizabeth Sibler of Swiss origin. She brought a consistent sense of purpose into my life at a time when, after six years' absence from the country of my birth, I felt out of place everywhere and at home nowhere. In 1968, I became Nobel laureate in medicine which I received with co-recipients, R.W. Holley and M.W. Nirenberg.

Hargobind Khorana

In 1960, Hargobind Khorana moved to the Institute for Enzyme Research at the University of Wisconsin and became a naturalised citizen of the United States. Since 1970, Khorana became the Alfred P. Sloan professor of biology and chemistry at the Massachusetts Institute of Technology.

I was born in La Chaux-de-Fonds, Switzerland. I left school when I was 13 to learn how to engrave watch-faces. My name at birth was Charles-Edouard Jeanneret. When I was 29, I went to Paris and adopted my maternal grandfather's name. While I was earlier a small-time architect, my new name saw me rising to great heights. As the world was going through a new age, I believed that architecture should also come of age and that "we must start again from zero".

I learnt architecture without much formal training. I travelled throughout Europe to see the different styles. Finally, when I settled in Paris, I met Ozenfant, who introduced me to ***purism***. I wrote several articles with him. I was particularly interested in city-planning. Many of my designs were rejected, but despite this I continued to influence others.

The new architectural style was called International Style and I propagated it relentlessly. I circulated manifestos, pamphlets, held exhibitions and had my own magazine. I wrote several books on interior decoration, painting and architecture which people could practically use. I loved formal dress and one could mostly see me only in dark suits, bow ties and horn-rimmed glasses. After the First World War, I built white-walled villas around Paris.

I loved ocean-liners and my work tried to capture the atmosphere of the open seas. Examples of my work are the Unité d'habitation, Marseilles, Chandigarh, India, the Swiss Dormitory in the Cité Universitaire in Paris and the Exposition Pavilion in Zürich. By 1950, I fell in love with heavier structures and my buildings began to have heavy walls and bright colour. I loved to work with RCC or reinforced concrete, which helped me try out new experiments.

Le Corbusier

Corbusier is known for his '*Five Points of Architecture*'. He was at his most influential in the sphere of urban planning because he was influenced by the problems of an industrial city that led to crowding and dirtiness. He was leader of the modernist movement to create better living conditions and a better society through his housing concepts.

I was born in La Jolla, California, to the town's only pharmacist. My parents divorced when I was six, but as a boy I continued to live in the seaside resort community with my mother and grandmother until age 10, when I was sent to St. John's Military Academy in Los Angeles. Upon graduating from the academy after 9th grade, I moved in with my father to San Diego, where as a teenager I attended the San Diego High School.

I studied at San Diego State University before switching over to studying medicine at the University of California, Berkeley. There I quickly realised that I was more interested in literature than in medicine. As an English major, I was persuaded to audition for a production of the film *Moby Dick*. Cast as Starbuck, I so fell in love with the theatre that shortly before graduation, I dropped out of school and caught the train for New York City.

I received a severe back injury, which kept me out of the war. With a scarcity of available actors, I was immediately cast in prime leading roles in films like *Keys of the Kingdom* (1944), *Spellbound* (1945), *Duel in the Sun* (1946) and *Gentleman's Agreement* (1947). Despite becoming a famous movie actor, I continued to devote time to the theatre, co-founding the prestigious La Jolla Playhouse in my hometown.

I was Hollywood's favourite action hero in war films such as *Pork Chop Hill*, *Roman Holiday* and *The Guns of Navarone*. But the apex of my career came in 1962, when I played Atticus Finch in *To Kill a Mockingbird*. For the film, I was awarded the Oscar for Best Actor. I won four Academy Award nominations in five years.

Gregory Peck

Gregory Peck was founder of the prestigious American Film Institute, three-time president of the Academy of Motion Picture Arts and Sciences, and a member of the National Council for the Arts. One of Hollywood's most popular actors, his life was as dignified as his most-notable film roles

I was born in 1932 to a school-teacher father in the small village of Chorwad in western Gujarat. I dreamt big even as a small boy, when I used to sell hot snacks to pilgrims outside a temple in my native village. And I did not stop dreaming big even when I went to Aden as a petrol-pump attendant at the age of 17, to help support my family. I returned to India in 1958, and started my first company in Bombay (now Mumbai)—a commodity trading and export house.

The company was set up with an investment of Rs 15,000. Today it is a conglomerate with an annual turnover of $13.2 billion. It is the only Indian private sector firm in the *Fortune 500* list. In the process, the company has also acquired one of the world's largest groups of shareholders, with over four million investors putting their faith in its stock.

In 1966, the group opened its first textile mill in Naroda near Ahmedabad. Two years later, the company went public, evoking a tremendous response from investors. Under my guidance, the corporation became one of the biggest first-generation success stories in Asia. I was voted by *Asiaweek* magazine amongst the 50 most powerful men in Asia—not once, but three times: in 2000, 1998 and 1996. The Federation of Indian Chambers of Commerce and Industry (FICCI) conferred on me the Indian Entrepreneur of the 20th Century Award.

I became known as a business tycoon and I summed up the secret of my remarkable success story by "think big, think fast and think ahead". My sons, Mukesh and Anil continued the trend after I passed away, with the mega launch of the GSM phone connection across India. After a prolonged dispute over division of Reliance Industries, Mukesh and Anil have parted company.

Dhirubhai Ambani

The group flagship, Reliance Industries, is valued by the market at nearly Rs 300 billion, while Reliance Petroleum commands a figure of nearly Rs 170 billion. The group's assets add up to over Rs 520 billion, and has five million individual shareholders. Dhirubhai became the highest-paid chief executive officer with an earning at Rs 88.5 million, leaving Wipro's Azim Premji far behind at Rs 42 million in a particular year.

I was born on November 27, 1940, in San Francisco, California. My father, a Hong Kong opera singer, had come with his wife and three children to USA in 1939. I appeared in his first film, *Golden Gate Girl*, at the age of three months. I appeared in roughly 20 films as a child actor. We then went back to Hong Kong. As a teenager, I became a member of a street gang, and began learning Kung-fu.

In 1959, after I landed in trouble for fighting, my mother sent me back to the US to live with family friends outside Seattle, Washington. I appeared in the television series *The Green Hornet*, which was aired from 1966 to 1967. I went on to make guest appearances in TV shows like *Ironside* and *Longstreet*, while my most notable role came in 1969, in the film *Marlowe*, starring James Garner.

Confronted with the dearth of meaty roles and the prevalence of stereotypes, especially for actors of Asian heritage, I left Los Angeles for Hong Kong in 1971, with my wife and two children. In Hong Kong, I signed a two-film contract. *Fists of Fury* was released in late 1971, featuring me as a vengeful fighter chasing the villains who had killed my **Kung-fu** master. I set new box-office records in Hong Kong. Those records were broken by my next film, *The Chinese Connection* (1972).

By the end of 1972, I was a major movie star in Asia. I founded my own production company, Concord Pictures, and released my first directorial feature, *Way of the Dragon*. My second directorial feature was my first major Hollywood project, *Enter the Dragon*. On July 20, 1973, just one month before the premiere of *Enter the Dragon*, I died in Hong Kong at the age of 32. *Enter the Dragon* went on to gross a total of over $200 million.

Bruce Lee

Lee finished high school in Edison, Washington, and enrolled as a philosophy major at the University of Washington. He taught the Wing Chun style of martial arts to his fellow-students and others. By 1964, he had opened his own martial arts school in Seattle. He opened two more schools in Los Angeles and Oakland. At his schools, he taught mostly a style which he called Jeet Kune Do.

I was born on or around May 21, 427 (or 428) BC in Athens, to Ariston and Perictione, both of Athenian aristocratic ancestry. I was given the finest education Athens had to offer and I devoted my considerable talents to politics and to writing of tragedy and other forms of poetry. I became a close associate of **Socrates**.

I welcomed the restoration of democracy, but my mistrust deepened some four years later when Socrates was tried on false charges and sentenced to death. I withdrew from Athens for a short time after Socrates' death and remained with Euclides in Megara. In 388-387 BC, I made my first trip abroad, to southern Italy and Syracuse. On my return to Athens, I began to teach in the Gymnasium Academe and soon afterwards acquired property nearby and founded my famous academy.

I wrote dialogues, which became the hallmark of my philosophical exposition. Socrates was the main character in these dialogues. My own great contribution was in the second group of writings. I introduced the doctrine of anamnesis (recollection). Since the soul is immortal and has at an earlier stage contemplated ideas, which are eternal and changeless truths of the Universe, humans do not learn, but remember.

My final group of works, written after 367, consists of the *Sophist*, the *Statesman*, *Philebus*, *Timaeus*, *Critias*, and the *Laws*. The *Laws*, my last work, once again takes up the question of the best framework in which a society might function for the betterment of its citizens. Here great stress is laid on an almost mystical approach to the great truth of the rational Universe.

Plato

Plato, who died in 347 BC, was the founder of an important philosophical school, which existed for almost 1,000 years. He was the most brilliant of Socrates many pupils and followers. His system attracted many followers in the centuries after his death to resurface as neo-Platonism— a great rival of early Christianity.

I was born on January 23, 1897 in a Bengali family of Cuttack as the 6th amongst eight sons and six daughters. I went to an English missionary school. I did not like the upmarket uniform, the formal mannerisms and the underlying foreignness of the environment and later shifted to a Bengali school. As a brilliant student, I was admitted to the Presidency College in Calcutta.

I was rusticated for my leadership role in violent defiance of an Englishman, Professor Otten, who treated Indian students with contempt, abuse and disdain. Barred from being admitted to any college or university, I met Sir Ashutosh Mukherjee, then Vice-Chancellor of Calcutta University, who gladly allowed me to enrol in the Scottish Church College.

On completion of a degree in philosophy, my father persuaded me to go to England to sit for the Indian Civil Service (ICS) exams on the ground that I needed to understand the British rulers and their methods more closely from within. I came in close contact with Bengali leader, C.R. Das. Inspired by the call of Mahatma Gandhi's *khadi* movement, I started selling *khaddar* (*dhoti* made of homespun cotton) in the streets of Calcutta.

Popularly known as Netaji, I came to occupy an honoured place in the history of India's Independence movement. At the outbreak of the Second World War, I visited Germany and came in touch with Hitler and other Italian and Japanese leaders to seek their assistance. I declared open war against the British rulers of India. I built up the Indian National Army (INA), which fought shoulder to shoulder against the allied forces in Burma and on the eastern front of India.

Subhas Chandra Bose

Subhas Chandra Bose told the Indians, "Give me blood and I will give you freedom." This was in direct conflict with Mahatma Gandhi's ideology. He disappeared suddenly and mysteriously after a meeting with Japanese Field-Marshal Terauchi in Saigon. According to official news, Netaji was killed in a plane crash somewhere near the Taihoku airport in 1945.

I was born Edda van Heemstra in Belgium on May 4, 1929. My father was an English banker and mother, a Dutch baroness. I grew up in England, but moved to the Netherlands after my parents separated. In 1948, I appeared in my first film, *Nederland in Lessen*. Following the Nazi invasion of the Netherlands in 1940, I was unable to leave the country until 1948, when I returned to London to study ballet on a scholarship at Arnhem Conservatory.

In 1949, I made my debut on the London stage in the chorus of High Button Shoes. I starred in the 1951 Broadway production *Gigi*, which garnered enormous critical acclaim. In 1953, I was cast as a runaway princess wooed by an international news journalist, played by Gregory Peck, in the romantic comedy *Roman Holiday*. My performance won me the Oscar for Best Actress; from then on, I became an international star and was considered the epitome of elegant chic.

I earned another **Oscar** nomination for Best Actress for the film *Sabrina*. In 1959, I received an Oscar nomination, the New York Film Critics Circle Award, and the British Film Academy Award for Best Actress for my role in *The Nun's Story*. I earned another Oscar nomination for *Breakfast at Tiffany's* (1961). My performance in *My Fair Lady* won Oscar and Golden Globe Award nominations; *Wait Until Dark* (1967) got a fifth Academy Award. My final role was in Steven Spielberg's *Always* (1989).

In 1988, I was named the official spokesperson for UNICEF. Among other honours, I was awarded the Cecil B. DeMille Award in 1990, the George Eastman Award for Lifetime Achievement, and the Screen Actors Guild Life Achievement Award in 1992. In 1993, I was presented the Council of Fashion Designers of America Award. Posthumous awards included the Jean Hersholt Humanitarian Award, a Grammy for Best Spoken Album for Children and the Women in Film Crystal Award.

Audrey Hepburn

As a film star, model and representative of humanitarian causes, Audrey Hepburn recieved over 50 other awards and international distinctions in films and later for her efforts on behalf of children worldwide. In 1992, Hepburn was diagnosed as suffering from colon cancer, for which she underwent surgery in Los Angeles; however, she died from the disease on January 20, 1993 in Tolochenaz, Switzerland.

I was born in Florence, Italy, on May 12, 1820, to wealthy parents. My father was heir to a Derbyshire estate. My mother, from solid merchant stock, devoted herself to the pursuit of social pleasures. I refused to marry several suitors, and at the age of 25 told my parents that I wanted to become a nurse. My parents were totally opposed to the idea as nursing was associated with working-class women.

My *Notes on Hospitals* (1859) detailed the proper arrangements necessary for civilian institutions. In the next year, I presided over the founding of a school for the training of nurses at St. Thomas' Hospital in London. In 1853, I became superintendent of the London, charity-supported, Institution for Sick Gentlewomen in Distressed Circumstances. In October 1854, I organised a group of 38 nurses, mostly from various religious orders, for service in the Crimean War.

Conditions at the British base hospital at Scutari were appalling and grew steadily worse as the flow of sick and wounded soldiers from the Crimean War rapidly increased. By the end of 1854, the death rate among patients fell by two-thirds. After 1858, I came to be recognised as a leading expert on military and civilian sanitation in India, and in which capacity I advocated irrigation as the solution to the problem of famine.

I left Scutari in the summer of 1856, soon after the hostilities ended. By now I had come to be idolised by the troops and the public as the 'Lady with the Lamp'. In *Notes on Matters Affecting the Health, Efficiency and Hospital Administration of the British Army* (1857) I used the experiences of the war as a body of data to prove the necessity for a new system. Within five years, this effort led to the reconstruction of the administrative structure of the War Office.

Florence Nightingale

Florence never recovered from the physical strain of the Crimean War. After 1861, she remained bedridden until her death on August 13, 1910. In 1895, she went blind. During the war, she received very little support until she used her contacts at *The Times* to report on the way the British Army treated its wounded soldiers. After a great deal of publicity, she was given the task of organising the barracks hospital where she dramatically reduced the death rate of her patients.

I was born in Paris on July 29, 1904, as the second child of my Parsi-Indian father and his French wife, Sooni. As a young boy, I spent my early years in Hardelot, a beach town in France, where my interest in flying was sparked off. I had varied interests—I desired to become a scholar at Cambridge, had a passion for fast cars, and served in a regiment called *Les Saphis* (The Sepoys) with the French Army in 1924.

I guided the destiny of India's largest business house for well over half a century. I pioneered civil aviation on the sub-continent, funded Homi Bhabha's ambition to catapult India into the Nuclear Age, laid the foundation of what would become the International Institute for Population Studies in 1956, and bank-rolled efforts to record and preserve for posterity the country's priceless folk arts. I also blueprinted development in the 'Bombay Plan' in 1944.

My passion for flying was fulfilled with the formation of the Tata Aviation Service in 1932. The first flight of Indian civil aviation took off at the Drigh Road airfield in Karachi on October 15, 1932, with me at the controls of the *Puss Moth* that I flew solo to Ahmedabad and onwards to Bombay. Post-Independence, Air-India International was formed as a joint sector company, with the government holding 49 per cent and the Tatas, 25 per cent share.

I arrived at the Tata group headquarters, Bombay House, to work under John Peterson, Director-in-Charge of Tata Steel, in 1925. In 1938, on the death of Sir Nowroji Saklatvala, Chairman of Tata Sons, I was catapulted to the head of India's largest industrial empire. I was barely 34-years old! R.M. Lala wrote my famous biography, *Beyond the Last Blue Mountain.*

J.R.D. Tata

Jehangir Ratanji Dadabhoy Tata, called JRD, by his friends, was awarded the Bharat Ratna in 1992. On his death on November 29, 1993, the Indian Parliament was adjourned in his memory. R. M. Lala, his biographer, writes: "As the evening mellows and the shadows lengthen, somewhere above in the sky, in an invisible *Puss Moth*, is a voyager still pressing ahead to cross beyond the last blue mountain where a glorious sunset awaits him."

I was born on May 5, 1818 in Trier, Rhenish Prussia, the son of Heinrich, a lawyer, and Henriette Presburg, a Dutchwoman. Barred from the practice of law for being a **Jew**, my father got converted to Lutheranism in about 1817, and I was baptised in the same church in 1824, at the age of six. I attended a Lutheran Elementary School but later became an atheist and materialist, rejecting both the Christian and Jewish religions. I said, "Religion is the opium of the people."

I attended the Friedrich Wilhelm Gymnasium in Trier for five years, before graduating in 1835, at the age of 17. In October 1835, I matriculated from Bonn University, where I attended courses primarily in jurisprudence. I then devoted myself primarily to philosophy. On April 15, 1841, the University of Jena awarded me a doctorate in philosophy for my thesis on *Difference between Democritean and Epicurean Natural Philosophy.*

In 1842, I became editor of the liberal Cologne newspaper, *Rheinische Zeitung*, which was suppressed by the Berlin government the following year. I moved to Paris, where I first came in contact with the working class, gave up philosophy as a life goal, and undertook a serious study of economics. In January 1845, I was expelled from France, so I moved to Brussels, where I lived until 1848. I founded the German Workers' Party and was active in the Communist League.

In 1848, my friend, Friedrich Engels and I published the famous *Manifesto of the Communist Party* (known as the *Communist Manifesto*). I finally settled in London, where I lived as a stateless exile, having been denied citizenship by both Britain and France. I spent most of my working time in the British Museum, doing research, both for my newspaper articles and books. In preparation for *Das Kapital*, I read virtually every available work in economic and financial theory of Europe.

Karl Marx

As philosopher, social scientist, historian and revolutionary, Marx is undoubtedly the most influential social thinker of the 19th century though he was ignored by the scholars of his time. Marx's excessive smoking and wine drinking, may have contributed to his illnesses. He died in London on March 14, 1883. He is buried in London's Highgate cemetery.

I was born on September 21, 1886 in Bromley, Kent. My father was a shopkeeper and a professional cricketer, and my mother served from time to time as a housekeeper at the nearby estate of Uppark. My father's business failed and I was apprenticed like my brothers to a draper, spending the years between 1880 and 1883 in Windsor and Southsea. Later I recorded these years in *Kipps* (1905).

My career as an author was fostered by an unfortunate accident as a child. I broke my leg and spent the mandatory rest period reading every book. I joined the Normal School of Science in London and studied biology under T.H. Huxley. However, my interest faltered. I taught in private schools before taking my B.S. degree in 1890. Next year I settled in London, married twice and in 1893 became a full-time writer.

As a novelist I made my debut with *The Time Machine* (1895), a parody of English class division and a satirical warning that human progress is not inevitable. The work was followed by science fiction as *The Island of Dr Moreau* (1896), *The Invisible Man* (1897) and *The War of the Worlds* (1898). *The First Men on the Moon* (1901) was a prophetic description of the methodology of space flight and *The War in the Air* (1908) describes a catastrophic aerial war.

Passionate concern for society led me to join the socialist Fabian Society in London, but I soon quarrelled with the society's leaders, among them being George Bernard Shaw. This experience was the basis for my novel *The New Machiavelli* (1911). After the First World War, I published several non-fiction works like *The Outline of History* (1920). My last book, *Mind at the End of its Tether* (1945), expressed pessimism about mankind's future prospects. I died in London on August 13, 1946.

H.G. Wells

English novelist, journalist, sociologist and historian, H.G. Wells is famous for his works of science fiction. Wells's best-known books are *The Time Machine* (1895), *The Invisible Man* (1897), and *The War of the Worlds* (1898). In his lifetime and after his death, Wells was considered a prominent socialist thinker.

I was born on July 31, 1880 in a village called Lamahi, about four miles (6 kms) from the city of Benares, to an ordinary working family. My father was a village postmaster. I lost my mother in my 7th year. My father married again. My early education was in a ***madrasa*** under a Maulvi, where I learnt Urdu. When studying in the 9th class, I was married much against my wishes. In 1919, while I was a teacher at Gorakhpur, I passed my B.A., with English, Persian and history.

I was forced to take on the family responsibilities in my 16th year. I gave up studies and got a government job as a village school teacher. My real name was Nawab Rai or Dhanpat Rai. My book *Soz-e-Watan* was banned by the then British government, which burned all the copies. Therefore, from 1910, I continued to write under a pen name. I married a widow named Shivarani Devi. I worked as a principal at a school in Kashi Vidyapeeth.

I was the first Hindi author to introduce realism in my writings. I pioneered the new art form—fiction with a social purpose. I wrote of the life around me and made my readers aware of the problems of the urban middle-class and the country's villages and their problems. I supplemented Gandhiji's work in the political and social fields by adopting his revolutionary ideas as themes for my literary writings.

My writings have been translated not only into all Indian languages, but also Russian, Chinese, and many other foreign languages. I spent my life as an ordinary school teacher, freedom fighter, social reformer, editor, and author of many great works. I left this world on October 8, 1936. Besides being a great novelist, I was also a social reformer and thinker. Literature, according to me, is a powerful means of educating public opinion.

Premchand

Premchand was a prolific writer. He has left behind a dozen novels and nearly 250 short stories. *Sevasadan* was his first novel. He believed in the principle: "Hate the sin and not the sinner." His best known novels are *Rangamanch*, *Gaban*, *Nirmala* and *Godan*. Three of his novels have been made into films.

I was born in Ithaca, New York, on August 11, 1921. I graduated from high school at the age of 15. I studied at State Teachers College in Elizabeth City, North Carolina, for two years, and joined the Coast Guard in 1939. In 1952, I became the first to hold the title of Coast Guard journalist. I used my writing talents to recount the old tales of sea-captains, which turned into my first published story.

In the 1950s, I served as a public relations officer, turning commonplace Coast Guard news into exciting, media-friendly narratives. After 20 years of service, I retired from the Coast Guard in 1959, to pursue a career as a full-time journalist. I wrote stories for *Playboy* and *Reader's Digest*, but my career created news in 1965 with the publication of *The Autobiography of Malcolm X.*

In 1965, I resolved to trace the genealogy of my mother's family. I had grown up listening to my grandmother's stories about 'Kin-tay', an African ancestor, who was enslaved and shipped to America. I embarked on a safari to Juffure, a village in Gambia, to learn more. A local historian was able to tell me about my great-great-great-great-grandfather, Kunta Kinte, who was brought to America via a slave-ship in 1767.

Roots, an account of my family's history, was published in 1976, after 12 years of research and creative reconstruction. *Roots* has been translated into 37 languages and has sold six million copies in hardcover and millions more in paperback. One year after the publication, ABC broadcast it as mini series *Roots: The Saga of an American Family*, and for which I received the Pulitzer Prize and the Spingarn Medal in 1977.

Alex Haley

Haley is credited with awakening an interest in genealogy, especially among African-American families. He created the Kinte Foundation to encourage preservation of African-American genealogical records. Haley's other works include *A Different Kind of Christmas* (1988), *Queen* (1993), and the television series *Palmerstown*, USA (1980). He died on February 10, 1992.

I was born in London, in a small flat above a shop in East Dulwich, as the eldest of three children. My father had a number of talents including watercolour painting, writing poetry, playing the piano. He taught himself foreign languages, and was a photographer. After working as a cutlery salesman, he joined his two older brothers in the family 'mantle warehousing' business of Fisher and Nephew. Theresa Mary Hamilton, my mother, did not approve of this.

My mother later moved with her children to Beckenham. Thomas, my father, established a successful wholesale clothing business in London, and sent regularly money to support his family. I started to write and send stories, articles, and poems to various periodicals. My first published poem, entitled *Have You* ? appeared in *Nash's Magazine* in 1917. My first book, *Child Whispers*, a collection of verse, appeared in 1922.

I was trained as a kindergarten teacher at Ipswich High School and opened my own infants' school. I later devoted myself entirely to writing. In 1926, I edited a new magazine for children, *Sunny Stories.* My stories, plays, and songs for *Teachers' World* gained popularity among the teachers. I also compiled a children's encyclopaedia. In the 1950s and 1960s I was attacked by critics and librarians who imposed sanctions on my writings owing to the books' limited vocabulary.

In 1938, I wrote my first full-length children's adventure story, *The Secret Island.* The idea of a fast-moving story, woven around familiar characters, proved to be very successful. The most popular became *The Famous Five*, *The Secret Seven*, the Adventure Series, the Mystery Series, and the Barney mystery books. I could write 10,000 words a day, which enabled her to keep her prodigious output.

Enid Blyton

In 1940, 11 books were published under her name, including *The Secret of Spiggy Holes*, which had appeared earlier in serial form in *Sunny Stories, Twenty-Minute Tales* and *Tales of Betsy May*—both collections of short stories, *The Children of Cherry Tree Farm*, and a story book annual for the *News Chronicle*. She is noted particularly for numerous series of books based on recurring characters and designed for different age groups.

Born on December 25, 1924 at Gwalior, Madhya Pradesh, I have with me a long parliamentary experience spanning over four decades. I have been a member of Parliament since 1957. I am the only parliamentarian elected from four different states at different times, namely Uttar Pradesh, Gujarat, Madhya Pradesh and Delhi. I was educated at Victoria College, Gwalior and DAV College, Kanpur.

I hold an M.A. (political science) degree and have many literary, artistic and scientific accomplishments to my credit. I edited *Rashtradharma* (a Hindi monthly), *Panchjanya* (a Hindi weekly) and the dailies *Swadesh* and *Veer Arjun.* My published works include *Meri Sansadiya Yatra*, *Meri Ikkyavan Kavitayen*, *Sankalp Kaal*, *Shakti-se-Shanti*, *Four Decades in Parliament*, 1957-95, *Lok Sabha mein Atalji* (a collection of speeches), *Mrityu ya Hatya*, *Amar Balidan*, etc.

I was conferred the Padma Vibhushan in 1992 in recognition of my services to the nation. I was also conferred the Lokmanya Tilak Puruskar, the Bharat Ratna Pandit Govind Ballabh Pant Award for the Best Parliamentarian in 1994. Earlier, the Kanpur University honoured me with an honorary doctorate of philosophy in 1993. I left my mark as the Minister for External Affairs from 1977-80 during which I gave an address in the United Nations in Hindi.

Elected leader of the National Democratic Alliance, which is a pre-election coming together of political parties from different regions of the country, I was earlier elected leader of my own Bharatiya Janata Party (BJP). This party emerged as the single largest party in the 13th Lok Sabha as was the case in the 12th Lok Sabha. I was also the first Prime Minister since Smt. Indira Gandhi to lead my party to victory in successive elections.

Atal Behari Vajpayee

Widely respected as a statesman of the genre of Pt. Jawaharlal Nehru, Shri Vajpayee's first stint in 1998-99 as Prime Minister has been characterised as 'one year of courage of conviction'. It was during this period that India entered a select group of nations following a series of successful nuclear tests at Pokhran in May 1998. He has said, "I have a vision of India: an India free of hunger and fear, an India free of illiteracy and want."

As a young student, at a rather severe missionary school in Madras, I first encountered the English language, and was immediately bewildered. Born in 1906, I was five-years old at the time and part of a middle-class Brahmin family of second-generation immigrants from rural South India. The family was new to the city, and still close to ancestral ways at home. I, as the only Brahmin boy in the class, came in for special mockery by the Christian teachers.

I was educated in Madras at Maharaja's College in Mysore. I lived in India ever since, apart from my travels. Most of my work, starting from my first novel *Swami and Friends* (1935) is set in the fictional town of **Malgudi**, which at the same time captures everything Indian while having a unique identity of its own.

I have published numerous novels, five collections of short stories (*A Horse and Two Goats*, *An Astrologer's Day*, *Lawley Road*, *Malgudi Days*, and *The Grandmother's Tale*), two travel books (*My Dateless Diary* and *The Emerald Route*), four collections of essays (*Next Sunday*, *Reluctant Guru*, *A Writer's Nightmare*, and *A Story-teller's World*), a memoir (*My Days*), and some translations of Indian epics and myths (*The Ramayana*, *The Mahabharata*, and *Gods, Demons and Others*).

In 1980, I was awarded the A.C. Benson Award by the Royal Society of Literature and was made an honorary member of the American Academy and Institute of Arts and Letters. In 1989 I was made a member of the Rajya Sabha (the non-elective House of Parliament in India). I received the Sahitya Akademi Award for *The Guide* (1958). In 2000 the Padma Vibhushan was conferred on me. I died in Chennai on May 13, 2002 at the age of 96.

R.K. Narayan

R. K. Narayan's full name is Rasipuram Krishnaswami Ayyar Naranayanaswami. In his early years, he signed his name as R. K. Narayanaswami, but at the time of the publication of *Swami and Friends*, he shortened it to R. K. Narayan on Graham Greene's suggestion. Autobiographical content forms a significant part of his novels.

I was born on July 18, 1918, in Transkei, South Africa. My father was a Xhosa chief in Transkei. I studied law at Witwatersrand University and set up practice in Johannesburg, in 1952. Unlike the young leaders with whom I grew up, I was ready to try every possible technique to end the policy of apartheid peacefully, though I, too, realised the futility of non-violence in view of the conditions that prevailed in my country.

I had joined the African National Congress (ANC) in 1944, at a time of political crisis. I was elected its president in 1951 and campaigned extensively for the repeal of discriminatory laws. I was appointed volunteer-in-chief in the resistance movement and subsequently banned for six months, before being sentenced to nine months in prison. I was arrested again during the state of Emergency following the Sharpeville shootings.

The All-African National Action Council came into being in 1961, and I was appointed its honorary secretary. I became head of Umkhonto weSizwe, which used sabotage in its fight against **apartheid**. I was tried in the Rivonia trial with other leaders of Umkhonto weSizwe on the charge of high treason and was given life sentence. During the 27 years in prison, my suffering put pressure on the apartheid government.

In 1982, I was moved to the maximum-security Pollsmoor prison outside Cape Town. I spent much of the next six years in solitary confinement. On February 11, 1990, I was out of Verster prison. In 1991, F. W. deKlerk and I led the negotiations for a democratic set-up in South Africa, and our efforts later won us the Nobel Peace Prize in 1993. In September 1992, we had signed a Record of Understanding that created a freely elected constitutional assembly.

Nelson Rolihlahla Mandela

After more than two decades as a prisoner, Mandela paved the way for an incredible transition of South Africa from apartheid to democracy. On April 27, 1994, in the first free elections, the ANC won over 62 per cent of the popular votes and Mandela was elected President of the country. He retired from the presidency in June 1999. In July 2001, Mandela was diagnosed as suffering from prostate cancer.

I was born on December 5, 1901 in Chicago, Illinois, and was the fourth of the five children. I became interested in drawing at an early age, selling my first sketches when I was only seven-years old. I was raised on a Midwestern farm in Marceline, Missouri, and in Kansas City, where I was able to acquire some rudimentary art instruction through correspondence courses at Saturday museum classes. I dropped out of high school at the age of 17 to serve in the First World War.

After the war, I took up a career as an advertising cartoonist. Here I created and marketed my first original **animated cartoons** and later perfected a method for combining live action and animation. In 1954, I successfully broke into television. On July 18, 1955, I opened the world's most popular amusement park in Anaheim, California, with 6.7 million people visiting it by 1966. In 1939, I received an honorary Academy Award and in 1954, I received four Academy Awards.

In 1965, President Lyndon B. Johnson presented me with the Presidential Medal of Freedom and the same year I was awarded the Freedom Foundation Award. My first feature-length film was *Snow White.* Other costly films followed, including *Pinocchio* and *Bambi*. In 1950, I started making live-action films like my biggest hit, *Mary Poppins*, with occasional animation to project wholesome, exciting stories full of fun and music.

I created Mickey Mouse in 1928 who made his debut in Steamboat Willie. He was first called Mortimer Mouse, then changed to Mickey on my wife's request. Mickey Mouse, Donald Duck, Minnie, and Goofy combined with innovative use of music and sound made my cartoon films a worldwide success. I, along with members of my staff, received more than 950 honours and citations from every nation in the world, including 48 Academy Awards and seven Emmys during my lifetime.

Walt Disney

Disney died on December 15, 1966. At the time of his death, his business was worth over $100 million a year, and the Disney studio had produced 21 full-length animated films, 493 short films, 47 live-action films, seven adventure features, 330 hours of Mickey Mouse television series, 78 half-hour Zorro television series, and 280 other television shows. He also created the California Institute of the Arts, known as Cal Arts.

I was born on December 30, 1975, in Orlando, Florida. My father was a retired Lieutenant Colonel in the US Army, and my mother, a Vietnamese. They introduced me to golf. At the age of eight, I won the first of six Optimist International Junior world titles. I won the US Junior Amateur Championships in 1991, 1992, and 1993, and the US amateur title in 1994, 1995, and 1996. I spent two years at Stanford University, where I won the NCAA title.

I turned pro in the summer of 1996. I won two titles and finished in the top 10, five times out of the first eight Professional Golf Association (PGA) tour events. In 1997, at the age of 21, I became the youngest player ever to win the Masters. In the same year, I was chosen the Associated Press Male Athlete of the Year and ESPN Male Athlete of the Year to became the youngest player ever to hold the No. 1 ranking in professional golf.

I was involved in a controversy in 2000 regarding filming a Buick commercial during the Screen Actors' Guild (SAG) strike. I won the third major event, the 2000 US Open, in California. As the No.1 ranked player in the world, I won the tournament by 15 strokes and broke the standard set by Tom Morris at the 1862 British Open. I then became the youngest player ever to win all four major titles: the PGA Championship, the Masters, the US Open, and the British Open.

I am the first person of African or Asian descent to win a major golf championship. With my victory at the American Express Championship on November 7, in Valderrama, Spain, I became the first golfer in 25 years to win eight PGA tour events in one year. I also shattered the previous single season winnings record by nearly $3 million, making myself the first player ever to break the $6 million mark with $6.6 million. My victories continue.

Tiger Woods

Nicknamed Tiger, he appeared on the Mike Douglas show at the age of two years, putting with Bob Hope. *Sports Illustrated* selected him as the 1996 and 2000 Sportsman of the Year. He was the first to win it more than once. L'Equipe selected him as the 2000 World Champion of Champions. He also had an actual scoring average in 2000 of 68.17 strokes, breaking Nelson's record of 68.33 strokes in 1945.

I was born on July 31, 1966 in a town in England called Chipping Sodbury. The name given to me at birth was Joanne Kathleen. My favourite book as a child was *The Little White Horse* by Elizabeth Goudge. My parents and sister Di and I moved twice while I was growing up. When I was nine-years old, my family moved to Tutshill, where I attended primary school, and later, the Wyedean Comprehensive. I was shy, freckly, with no natural flair for athletics.

I attended Exeter University where I studied French. When 26-years old, I moved to Portugal to be an English teacher. I taught in the afternoons and evenings, so that I could be free to work on my writing during the mornings. I met and married a journalist in Portugal, and our daughter, Jessica, was born in 1993. Shortly after the birth of our daughter, we divorced, and I moved with my daughter to Edinburgh, Scotland.

I requested for a grant from the Scottish Arts Council, which was eventually granted, in order to complete my book. When it was completed, after several rejections, I sold it to Bloomsbury in the UK for about $4,000. To maintain my daughter and myself, I began to work as a French teacher. After several months, Arthur A. Levine of Books/Scholastic Press bought the American rights to the book and I received enough money to give up teaching and write full time.

With over 170 million books sold, my books have been translated into 55 languages and distributed in over 200 countries. All my six books are currently on bestseller lists in the United States, Britain, and around the globe. My latest book created records when it sold out. I won the Hugo Award, the Bram Stoker Award, the Whitbread Award for best children's book and a special commendation for the Anne Spencer Lindbergh Prize.

J. K. Rowling

Rowling is the author of Harry Potter books. When she was a child, in one of their homes, close to Bristol, and in Winterbourne, she had friends next door whose last name was Potter. She never forgot the children, or the last name, which she liked very much.

I was born on June 10, 1955, in Bangalore. My father was secretary of the Mysore Badminton Association for many years. In my first tournament, in September 1962, I lost in the first round and refused to leave the court, howling at the top of my voice. I relented only when the president of the Association promised me a new racquet. Two years later, I won the state junior championship. At 15 years of age, I made a record by winning the junior boys' and men's singles badminton titles in 1971.

In 1980, I won the Badminton Grand Slam for winning three major international badminton tournaments, including the All-England Badminton Championship. I won the Nationals nine years in a row (1971-1979), but did not play again in the Nationals till 1989. At the Commonwealth Games in 1978, I won the gold medal. I trained in Indonesia for several months in 1979; this was probably what gave me an edge in fitness that Indian players often lack.

In 1980, I won the Danish Open and the Swedish Open. Seeded 3rd at the All-England, I beat Morten Frost in the semi-finals and Liem Swie King in the finals in straight games. In 1981, at the All England Championship, I was seeded 6th, although I was the defending champion. I beat the legendary Rudy Hartono in three games in the semi-finals. In the finals, I was pitted against Liem Swie King again, but this time I lost in all the three games.

In 1982, I turned pro and moved to Denmark because of the better training facilities. I retired from competitive play in 1991. I became the coach of the Indian national team for the Thomas Cup in 1993 and 1996. I started an academy for training badminton players in Bangalore. I even tried to improve the administration of the game by forming an organisation parallel to the Badminton Association of India. The two associations are now merged. I received the Arjuna Award in 1972.

Prakash Padukone

Padukone won about 15 international titles in the first half of the 1980s. In 1971, at Jabalpur, a young Prakash Padukone watched in awe the legendary Indonesian, Rudy Hartono, who became his hero. In the Swedish Open of 1980, he beat Rudy Hartono 9-15, 15-12 and 15-1. "I could have beaten him on 'love' in the last game, but I did not have the heart to do that to my idol. So I ensured that he got one point before I beat him," Padukone said.

Born in Karnal, India and hailing from a family that owned a local rubber manufacturing plant, I was the youngest of four children. I studied at the Tagore Bal Niketan. Sanjay, my brother, was my sole mentor. His plans of being a commercial pilot were shattered when his medical reports were not up to the mark. In 1982, I became the first woman to graduate in aeronautical engineering from the Punjab Engineering College. I happened to be the only girl in the aeronautics batch.

While getting my degree, I read a book about the famed Lockheed Skunkworks plant in California, where new space vehicles are designed. I applied to American schools for advance degree and stay in the United States. I moved to the US and earned a masters degree from the University of Texas in 1984. Later, I earned a doctorate from the University of Colorado. There, I met Professor C.Y. Chow, who had a job available for doing NASA research in complex fluid dynamics.

I began to work on aircraft physics at NASA's Ames Research Center in 1988, after completing my doctoral studies. I became an American citizen in 1990 and in 1993 joined Overset Methods Inc. as a vice president to study aerodynamics. In 1994, I was chosen as an astronaut. I made my first spaceflight in 1997 on a **shuttle mission** that did research on the effects of weightlessness, studied the sun's outer atmosphere and retrieved a science satellite.

I married flight instructor Jean-Pierre Harrison. I got inspiration to take up flying from J.R.D. Tata. One of the seven asteroids discovered at the Palomar Observatory in 2001 has been named after me. I served as Flight Engineer and Mission Specialist 2 on the Columbia Space Shuttle that got destroyed on February 1, 2003, on re-entry into the atmosphere, 16 minutes before landing.

Kalpana Chawla

Kalpana said in an interview before going on her last space flight: "Just looking at Earth, looking at the stars during the night part of Earth, just looking at our planet roll by and the speed at which it goes by and the awe that it inspires; just so many such good thoughts come to your mind when you see all that. Doing it again is like living a dream—a good dream—once again."

I was born into a high caste Brahmin family. My roots made me immensely proud of Hindu history and culture. As I grew up, I developed my sense of free thinking. I did not believe in having a blind allegiance to any political or religious following. I later went on to become a member of the Hindu right wing organisation, i.e. Rashtriya Swayamsevak Sangh (RSS) and of the Hindu Mahasabha. Both organisations were extremely hostile towards Mahatma Gandhi and the Muslims.

I was an active worker against the eradication of untouchability and the caste system. I believed that irrespective of one's background, one should be judged purely on the basis of merit. I personally organised anti-caste dinners in which thousands of Hindus of different castes participated. I grew up reading speeches and writings of Dadabhai Naroji, Vivekananda, Gopal Krishna Gokhale, and Balgangadhar Tilak. I studied the tenets of socialism and Marxism. I also studied Veer Savarkar's ideology. He was the leader of the right-wing extremists.

I was a militant activist, highly critical of Mahatma Gandhi and the Indian National Congress. I was against Gandhi's ideology behind the formation of the doctrine of *ahimsa* and non-violence. I wrote articles denouncing Gandhi and the Congress Party. On January 13, 1948, Mahatma Gandhi decided to fast unto death protesting against the Indian government's decision to withold the transfer of Rs 550 million to the Government of Pakistan, as per the Partition agreement.

I found Mahatma Gandhi's resolve harmful for the 'Hindu nation'. I believed he had a 'pro-Muslim bias'. I assassinated the Mahatma after bowing to him in reverence at his daily prayer meeting in New Delhi on January 30, 1948. On November 8, 1948, I was allowed to make my public statement in order to explain as to why I had killed Gandhi. For this I had prepared a thesis that was a 90-page manuscript. They sent me to the gallows on November 15, 1949.

Nathuram Vinayak Godse

Nathuram Godse assassinated Mohandas Karamchand Gandhi, who is considered the Father of the Indian Nation. Shortly after he was shot to death with his hands still folded in greeting, the Mahatma cried: '*Hey Ram! Hey Ram!*'. The Supreme Court of India found Godse and his associate Narayan Apte guilty and sentenced them to death.

Born in September, 1915, in Pandharpur, Maharashtra, my mother, Zunaib died in my infancy and my father remarried and moved to Indore. It was in Indore that I went to school. I moved to Mumbai at the age of 20, when I was admitted to the J. J. School of Arts. I married in 1941. In the 1947 annual exhibition of the Bombay Art Society, my painting *Sunhera Sansaar* was shown. This was my first exhibition.

Soon after the Partition of India, a Progressive Artists' Group was formed. Through it, I was exposed to the works of Emile Nolde and Oskar Kokoschka. From 1948 to 1950, a series of exhibitions all over India brought my work to the notice of the public. During my early days in Mumbai, I earned money by painting cinema hoardings. I was paid four or six annas per square foot by the New Theatres distributor.

I tried other jobs as well. One of the best paying was a toy factory, where I designed and built fretwork toys. In 1952, I had my first solo exhibition in Zurich, and over the next few years my work was widely seen in Europe and the USA. In 1966, I was awarded the Padmashri. A leading industrialist created news by buying hundreds of my paintings for a whopping Rs100 crores. I am also known as a barefooted artist. I became famous for my paintings of horses.

In the following year, I made my first film, *Through the Eyes of a Painter.* It was shown at the Berlin Festival and won the award, the Golden Bear. Some of my best known works are Sufi paintings, first exhibited at the Pundole Gallery in 1978. In the 1990s, I began to admire the beautiful Hindi film actress Madhuri Dixit, and made a movie with her in the lead. In 2003, I made another film *Meenaxi*, with another Indian actress.

Maqbool Fida Hussain

Hussain's famous exhibition includes his Shwetambari exhibition at the Jehangir Art Gallery, which consisted of two halls shrouded in white cloth. At the Tata Centre in Kolkata, for several days he painted pictures of six goddesses. On the last day of the exhibition, he destroyed his paintings by painting over them with white. He was nominated to the Rajya Sabha in 1987; and during his six-year term he produced the Sansad portfolio.

I was born into an illustrious family in Calcutta in 1921. My grandfather, Upendra Kishore Ray Chaudhary, was a publisher, musician and creator of children's literature in Bengali. My father was a noted satirist and writer of nonsense rhymes. I was well educated and spent many years as a layout artist in a publishing house. I first worked in the advertising industry as a major graphic designer, and designed hundreds of book jackets. I illustrated my own books.

Inspired by the novel *Pather Panchali*, I decided to make it into a film and shot it on location using friends as actors, putting up the funding myself. The film was successful both artistically and commercially, winning notice at the 1956 Cannes Film Festival and proving a boon to the Indian film industry. I went on to make two more movies: *Aparajito* in 1957, followed by *Apur Sansar* in 1960.

Contemporaneous with these films were two staggering films: *Devi* (The Goddess) and *Jalsaghar* (The Music Room), on the ways of the landed aristocracy in Bengal and its decline. My later films were more contemporary like *Nayak* in 1966, *Pratiwandi* in 1970, *Seemabaddha* in 1971, *Jana Aranya* in 1975. With my film *Shatranj ke Khiladi* (1977), based on a short story by the famous Hindi writer Premchand, I ventured into the terrain of mid-19th century India, to depict the 'clash of cultures'.

I created for children *Gopi Gyne Bagha Byne*, which soon gained a cult following in Bengal. I was a profilic short story writer, with over a dozen volumes to my credit; and I contributed regularly to the children's journal *Sandesh*, which I also edited. In Bengal, particularly in Calcutta, where no respectable intellectual could be other than a Marxist, I was charged with being a supreme representative of bourgeois culture.

Satyajit Ray

In the pantheon of world cinema, Ray is one of the most illustrious figures. He succeeded in making Indian cinema for the first time in its history as something to be taken seriously by the rest of the world. He won the Dadasaheb Phalke Award in 1985, the Academy's Lifetime Achievement Award (Oscar) and also the Bharat Ratna in 1992, apart from awards at Cannes, Venice and Berlin.

I was born in Mysore in South India on July 9, 1925. I had my early education in Calcutta before doing basic training with dance-maestro Uday Shankar, after which I joined the Prabhat Studios. It was here that I got a break as a choreographer with the film *Hum Ek Hain* (1946), the launching pad of friend-and-actor Dev Anand. From Prabhat I moved on to Famous Studios and then on to Bombay Talkies.

The year 1951 saw the release of *Baazi*, my directorial debut. Its songs were sung mainly by well-known playback singer of the times, Geeta Roy, with whom I fell in love and married her on May 26, 1953. *Baaz* in 1953 saw me make my debut as leading hero. *Aar Paar*, released in 1954, established me as a director to reckon with. Followed some of my best works: *Mr and Mrs 55*, *Pyaasa* and *Kaagaz ke Phool* but the last mentioned was a dismal failure at the box-office.

I continued to produce films and act in both home and outside productions. But never did I ever give my name in the credits as director again. *Sahib Bibi aur Ghulam* though credited to writer Abrar Alvi bears my unmistakable stamp. The film won the President's silver medal as well as the Film of the Year Award from the Bengal Film Journalists Association.

However, my personal life was in shambles. I had separated from my wife allegedly due to my involvement with my discovery and leading actress Waheeda Rehman. On October 10, 1964, I took an overdose of sleeping pills and committed suicide though doubts linger as to whether my death was accidental. It was said that with my death, Indian cinema had lost one of its greatest geniuses.

Guru Dutt

It was Guru Dutt who revolutionalised the close up shot. He went into closer magnifications of characters as if probing for their internal feelings. He strongly felt that 80 per cent of acting was done through the eyes and 20 per cent in the form of body language. His thematic contents coupled with his technical innovations made his films the masterpieces they are.

I was born Annie Wood to Dr William Wood and Emily Morris in Clapham, London, in 1847. After my father died when I was just five-years old, my mother had to struggle to make both ends meet. Her friend, Ellen Marryat, a strict Calvinist, took full responsibility of my education. My education also involved travelling within Europe. In 1867, at the age of 19, I married a young clergyman, Rev. Frank Besant. By the age of 23, I had a daughter and a son.

When I started developing unorthodox religious views, free thinking and refused to attend communion, my husband ordered me to leave our home. After we got legally separated in 1873, I completely renounced Christianity and in 1874, I joined the National Secular Society and the Fabian Society whose noted members were George Bernard Shaw and Walter Crane. I edited the *National Reformer* along with Charles Bradlaugh that would advocate radical thinking such as birth control, trade unions, national education and women's right to vote.

I was charged with 'obscene libel' after I wrote a book *The Fruits of Philosophy*, advocating birth control. Soon afterwards I wrote another book on the same subject, titled *The Laws of Population*. In 1889 I wrote an article for the influential book *Fabian Essays*. I wrote and spoke against dangerous industrial working conditions and low remuneration for young factory women. When I was elected as a member of the London School Board, I initiated the free meals for undernourished children and free medical examination programme.

After I joined the *Theosophical Society* founded by Madame Blavatsky, a spiritualist, I proceeded on my mission to spread theosophical beliefs all around the world, especially in India. Here, I continued to fight for women's rights. I founded the Central Hindu College at Varanasi. I presided over the Indian Home Rule League that worked to gain freedom of the country from the British. Interned during the First World War, I presided over the National Congress in 1917 and was elected as the General Secretary of the National Convention of India in 1923. I died in Madras, in 1933.

Annie Besant

Mahatma Gandhi lauded Annie Besant with 'awakening India from her deep slumber'. A great orator and writer, one of her famous quotes was: "Never forget that life can only be nobly inspired and rightly lived if you take it bravely and gallantly, as a splendid adventure in which you are setting out into an unknown country, to face many a danger, to meet many a joy, to find many a comrade, to win and lose many a battle."

I was born as Agnes Gonxha Bojaxhiu on August 26, 1910, in Skopje, Macedonia. At the tender age of 12, I decided to take up the vocation of a Christian missionary in aiding the poor. When I turned 18, I joined the Sisters of Loretto, an Irish community of nuns with mission in Calcutta, after being trained in Dublin. I was a teacher and principal of St. Mary's High School in Calcutta for 17 years. I left the convent to work for the poorest of poor in the slums of Calcutta.

Soon I opened an open-air school for children where I was assisted by many volunteers and enough funds were available. On October 7, 1950, I initiated my own order, The Missionaries of Charity with 12 members, which later grew to more than 4,000 nuns. It took to caring and loving the poor, the outcast, the sick and the underprivileged by running orphanages, AIDS hospices and various charity centres spread all over the world—the former Soviet Union, East European countries, Asia, Africa and Latin America.

We would undertake relief work in countries that had been hit by natural catastrophes such as floods, epidemics and famines. In 1952, I established a home, ***Nirmal Hriday*** for dying destitutes so that they would be taken care of and would die with dignity. In 1979, I won the Nobel Peace Prize. I would wear a $1 worth white sari so that I could identify myself with the poor. Pope Paul VI gifted me a white Lincoln Continental, which I auctioned to raise money to build a leprosarium outside Calcutta.

I was criticised for my thoughts on anti-abortion and divorce. In 1982, in the middle of the siege in Beirut, I rescued 37 children trapped in a hospital by convincing both the Israeli army and Palestinian guerillas to temporarily cease-fire. I was awarded the Pope John XXIII Peace Prize in 1971, and the Nehru Prize in 1972, for promoting international peace and understanding. I also received the Balzan Prize in 1979 and the Templeton and Magsaysay awards.

Mother Teresa

She was called 'Mother Teresa' for her selfless work for the poor and the outcast. After her death, French President Jacques Chirac commented: "This evening, there is less love, less compassion, less light in the world." Mother Teresa was formally beatified by Pope John Paul II in 2003 with the title 'Blessed Teresa of Calcutta'.

I was born on January 27, 1756, at Salzburg. My father, Leopold, was a noted composer. Together with my sister, Nannerl, I received intensive musical training. By the age of six, I was already composing and had become an accomplished piano performer. In 1762, my father presented me at the Imperial Court in Vienna, and from 1763 to 1766, my sister and I undertook continuous musical tours across Europe. I was the most famous child prodigy on a keyboard at that time.

When I was 12, I produced my first real operas: the *German Singspiel*, *Bastien und Bastienne*, and the opera *Buffa la Finta Semplice.* When I was 14, I went to Italy to become an opera composer. During those years, I produced my first large-scale settings of *opera seria.* At 19, I wrote nine symphonies (Nos. 22-30) and all my six concertos for violin. In 1780, I got a commission from Munich for the opera *Seria Idomeneo,* one of my greatest works.

From the age of 25 till I died at 35, I composed six symphonies, including the famous last three: No. 39 in E-flat Major, No. 40 in G Minor, and No. 41 in C Major. I finished these three works within six weeks in 1788. My three greatest Italian operas are *Le nozze di Figaro* (1786), *Don Giovanni* (1787), and *Cosi fan tutte* (1790). My last project was the *Requiem*.

Other chamber music composed by me includes the two piano quartets, seven late violin sonatas, the last piano trios, and the piano quintet with winds, the last string quintets and the clarinet quintet. I also composed the last 17 of the piano concertos, almost all for my own performance. They represent one of my greatest achievements, with their formal mastery, their subtle relationships between piano and orchestra and their combination of lyricism and symphonic growth.

Wolfgang Amadeus Mozart

Wolfgang Amadeus Mozart died on December 5, 1791. He died in complete penury and was given a third-class funeral. At his death from a feverish illness that gave rise to much speculation (he was not poisoned), he left unfinished the *Requiem*, his first large-scale work for the church since the C Minor Mass of 1783, also unfinished. Mozart was buried in a Vienna suburb, with little ceremony and in an umarked grave.

I was born as Edson Arantes do Nascimento on October 23, 1940, in Três Coracoes, Brazil. At the age of nine, I dropped out of school so that I could pursue my dream of becoming a professional player. I earned money as a cobbler's apprentice, while my father coached me in soccer. As a teenager I began playing for a local league club. I remained on the team for four years (1950-54), and during my last season, emerged as the club's most renowned team member.

I became a 17-year old sensation on the Brazilian national team to the 1958 World Cup Final. I scored two dramatic goals that resulted in a 4-2 win over Sweden. Brazil won the World Cup Championship, and I gained international recognition for my masterful performance in the series. In 1962, Brazil captured the title for the second time, and, in 1970, they took home the coveted Jules Rimet Trophy for their third World Cup victory.

I announced my retirement in 1974, but a year later I was offered a $7 million contract to play with the New York Cosmos of the North American Soccer League (NASL). While with the Cosmos, I was named the 1976 NASL Most Valuable Player. I led the Cosmos to the League Championship in 1977, and succeeded in making soccer a more visible sport in the US.

When I retired in 1978, I held a record of 1,280 goals in 1,362 games—a record only surpassed by fellow-Brazilian, Arthur Friedenreich. In 1978, I received the International Peace Award. In 1977, I published a best-selling autobiography, *My Life and the Beautiful Game*. I featured in many documentaries, and have composed many musical pieces. In 1999, I was named the Athlete of the Century by the National Olympic Committee, thus outshining Olympic greats like Muhammad Ali, Carl Lewis and Michael Jordan.

Pele

Former Brazilian football player, Pele scored over a thousand goals in his career. He was also famous for his lightning speed and his strength on the ball. In December 1994, President-elect Fernando Henrique Cardoso appointed him to the Special Secretariat for Sports in the Brazilian cabinet. In 1997, Pelé received an honorary British knighthood. His name literally means 'Black Pearl'.

I was born on March 14, 1879, in Ulm, Germany. I grew up in Munich, where my father, Hermann, owned a small electrochemical factory. After failing in my first entrance examination to the prestigious Swiss Federal Institute of Technology in Zurich, I gained admittance in 1896 and began my four years, studying physics and mathematics.

After graduation in 1900, I became a naturalised Swiss citizen in 1901 and got a job as a technical assistant at the Swiss Patent Office in Bern. In 1903, I married my university sweetheart, Mileva Maric. In 1905, I published an article entitled 'A New Determination of Molecular Dimensions' in the well-known German physics monthly, *Annalen der Physik*. The article earned me a Ph.D. from the University of Zurich.

I worked as a professor of physics at universities in Prague and Zurich before moving to Berlin in 1914 with my wife and two sons. I took up a post at the Prussian Academy of Sciences, where I could continue with research and lecture at the University of Berlin. Unhappy with life in Berlin, my wife Mileva returned to Switzerland with the sons, before the beginning of the First World World. We divorced in 1919. I remarried my second cousin, Elsa Lowenthal, later that year.

In 1915, I perfected my general theory of relativity, summing up this theory with the mathematical equation $E=mc^2$. My findings on relativity were published as *The Principle of Relativity*, *Sidelights on Relativity*, and *The Meaning of Relativity*. In November 1919, the Royal Society of London announced that their experiment conducted during the solar eclipse of that year had confirmed the predictions I had made in my theory and in 1921, I was awarded the Nobel Prize in physics.

Albert Einstein

Known as the greates scientist of the 20th century, he proposed the Theory of Relativity and made major contributions to the development of quantum mechanics, statistical mechanics and cosmology. In 1933, he renounced German citizenship and migrated to America. He died on April 18, 1955, at the age of 76.

I was considered the pioneer of the Indian film industry. I hailed from Nasik and was born on April 30, 1870 in Trimbakeshwar. I devoted my life to making silent movies. I had a multifaceted personality. I was a student of Sir J.J. School of Arts, Bombay and Kalabhavan of Baroda. After passing out from the art school, I saw a movie on the life of Jesus Christ, which inspired me to make an experimental movie in India.

I worked in a photographic studio at Ratlam and learned three-colour block making and ceramics. Raising a loan from an old friend and pledging his life insurance, I sailed for England on February 1, 1912 to purchase the necessary equipment and acquaint myself with the technical aspects of film-making. After two weeks in London, I returned with a Williamson camera, a perforating machine, developing and printing equipment and some raw stock.

Starting with the famous movie on mythological character *Raja Harishchandra* in 1913, I made 95 movies and 26 short films in the span of 19 years, till 1932. I earned a lot of money, but ploughed it back in the industry. When I stepped into this venture, no one had anticipated this industry to flourish so much that thousands of people would be able to earn their livelihood from it, nor did anyone foresee the amount of huge money transactions involved in it.

In 1932, movies got voice. The age of silent movies receded back. My last silent movie *Setubandhan* was released in 1932 and the same movie was again released by dubbing the voice. Later on, I made my only talkie which was not successful. That was the time when I retired from the film industry. Talkies won over the silent movies and this affected the silent movie business adversely. I died in 1944, a forgotten man.

Dadasaheb Phalke

Phalke will always remain the founder of the world's largest film industry. He was, however, not a practical man and could never do financially successful business. His health also did not cooperate in the later stages of his life. Today the most prestigious award of the Indian film industry, the 'Dadasaheb Phalke Award' is named after him.

Glossary

P. 1

Sparta: Sparta, a city-state, was the greatest military power of Greece and played a catalytic role in her history. The later Sparta did not produce art or philosophy, neither left us any written work, but its people were admired for their valour and for keeping alive the Greek values.

Antagonistic suitor: Unfriendly or difficult-to-please woman for a man to marry.

Achilles: Achilles, in Greek mythology, foremost Greek hero of the Trojan war, son of Peleus and Thetis. He was a formidable warrior possessing fierce and uncontrollable anger.

Bard: Literally, a poet.

P. 2

Pharaoh: The title of the kings of ancient Egypt.

Venus Genetrix: The temple of Venus Genetrix was made of solid marble, almost square, Corinthian, with eight columns across the front (octastyle) set very close together (pycnostyle) and eight down each side (peripheral).

Asp: A small poisonous snake in North Africa. It was a symbol of royalty in ancient Egypt.

P. 3

River Nile: The longest river in the world, flowing for about 6,677 km (4,150 miles) through eastern Africa from its most remote source in Burundi to a delta on the Mediterranean Sea in northeast Egypt.

Palace of Nabukodonossor: The palace of Nabukodonossor was in Babylonia where King Alexander died.

P. 4

Magadha: Ancient Indian kingdom lying within a part of of Bihar and Jharkhand. Its capital was Pataliputra (now Patna). The kingdom rose to prominence in the mid 7th century BC.

Chandragupta Maurya: Chandragupta Maurya was the first king of the Maurya dynasty. His mother's name was Mur, so he was called Maurya. Chandragupta Maurya ruled for 34 years (1541-1507 BC).

Pataliputra: Pataliputra, the ancient name for Patna, was a great centre of learning and produced eminent world-class scholars; it was the seat of power and nerve centre of the Mauryan empire.

Kalinga: Kalinga was an ancient kingdom of central-eastern India, in the province of Orissa. It was conquered by the Mauryan emperor, Ashoka around 260 BC.

P. 5

Mongols: Asian people, numbering about six million and distributed mainly in the Republic of Mongolia, the Inner Mongolian Autonomous Region of China, and of Kalmykia and the Buryat Republic of Russia.

Great Wall of China: A line of fortifications extending for about 2,414 km (1,500 miles) across northern China. Built in the 3rd century BC by some 3,00,000 labourers (mainly criminals, conscript soldiers and slaves), the wall proved ineffective against invaders and is today a major tourist attraction.

P. 6
Bhagwad Gita: The *Bhagwad Gita* (the blessed Lord's song) is a 700-verse section of the *Mahabharata* and occurs just before the great battle between the Kauravas and Pandavas. It is written as a conversation between Arjuna and Lord Krishna, the statesman-god. The path, as laid down by the *Bhagwad Gita*, is still considered an ideal way of life by Indians.
Sabarmati Ashram: Sabarmati Ashram, also known as Gandhi Ashram, is on the western banks of Sabarmati river in northern Ahmedabad. This *ashram* was earlier established in the Kochrab area of Ahmedabad in 1915. In 1917 it was shifted to the banks of Sabarmati river.
Mahatma: A person with a 'great soul'.

P. 7
Monarch: A king or queen. Britain's head of state is a constitutional monarch (with limited ruling power).
Asterix comic books: Asterix comics are fun-filled adventures taking place in the time of Gaul and the rule of Caesar. Starring Asterix and his best friend Obelix, these hilarious comics are about the rivalry between Caesar and the witty villagers.

P. 8
Tartars: Turkish-speaking people living primarily in Russia. They number about 5.5 million and are largely Sunni Muslims. The name is derived from Tata or Dada, a Mongolian tribe that inhabited the present north-east Mongolia in the 5th century. First used to describe the people that overran parts of Asia and Europe under Mongol leadership in the 13th century; it was later extended to include almost every Asian nomadic invader. Before the 1920s, the Russians used the name Tartar to designate the Azerbaijani Turks and several tribes of the Caucasus.

P. 9
American War of Independence: The American Revolutionary War (1775-1783), also known as the American War of Independence, was fought primarily between Great Britain and revolutionaries within 13 of her North American colonies. The war, which spread far beyond British North America, resulted in the overthrow of British rule and establishment of the United States of America.
Electoral College: A group of people whose job is to choose a political or religious leaders.

P. 10
Baptist: Baptist is a denomination of Protestant Christians holding a distinctive belief with regard to the ordinance of baptism.
Kansas-Nebraska Act: Bill that became law on May 30, 1854, by which the US Congress established the territories of Kansas and Nebraska.

P. 11
Harrow: Harrow, the outer borough of Greater London, grew foodstuffs for London. It is mainly residential and contains parts of the Green Belt areas set aside as parkland. Optical and photographic goods and glass are manufactured here.
Sandhurst Royal Military College: The Royal Military Academy, Sandhurst (commonly known as Sandhurst) is the British army officers' training centre.
House of Commons: The lower house of Parliament of Britain. It includes

representatives from England, Northern Ireland, Scotland and Wales, all elected by the people. It is more powerful than the House of Lords, the upper house of Parliament. The leader of the ruling party in the House of Commons is Britain's Prime Minister who chooses a cabinet composed mainly of members of the House of Commons.

P. 12
Pokhran: Pokhran is a remote location in the Thar desert region in the Indian state of Rajasthan. Pokhran is the test site for India's nuclear programme. The Atomic Energy Commission of India detonated its first underground nuclear weapon here on May 18, 1974. The Indian government conducted five nuclear tests on May 11 and May 13, 1998. Since then, India has declared a moratorium on nuclear testing.

P. 13
Eureka: Archimedes is said to have shouted "*Eureka!*" ("I have found it!") as he stepped into his bath and realised that the volume of an object could be measured by determining the amount of water it displaces.

P. 14
Royal Mint: The Royal Mint is the body permitted to make (mint) coins in the United Kingdom. The Royal Mint originated over 1,000 years ago, but it has functioned since 1975 as a Government Trading Fund, operating in much the same way as a government-owned company. It not only mints coins for the UK, but also mints and exports coins to many other countries. It also produces military medals, commemorative medals and other such items for governments, schools and businesses.
Three Laws of Motion: In 1665 and 1666, Isaac Newton developed three laws that describe all the states of motion — rest, constant motion and accelerated motion. The laws also explain how forces cause all the states of motion. Rest is the state of an object with no movement. Constant motion is the state of an object at a constant velocity. Accelerated motion is the state of an object whose rate of acceleration changes after a state of constant motion.

P. 16
Raman Effect: Raman Effect is the appearance of additional lines in the spectrum of monochromatic light that is scattered by a transparent material medium. The effect was discovered by C. V. Raman in 1928. Raman spectrometry is a useful technique in physical and chemical research, particularly for the characterisation of materials.
Bharat Ratna: The Bharat Ratna is India's supreme decoration and honour awarded for the highest degree of national service. This service includes artistic, literary, and scientific achievements, as well as "recognition of public service of the highest order". Unlike knights, holders of the Bharat Ratna carry no special title, but they do hold a place in the order of precedence.

P. 17
Madame Tussaud's Wax Museum: Statues of well-known celebrities are cast in wax and displayed at Madame Tussaud's museum.

P. 18
Kapellmeister: A Kapellmeister is the director or conductor of an orchestra or choir. When used today, it suggests involvement in orchestra or choir policy (for example,

selecting repertoire, concert schedules, choosing guest conductors and so on) as well as conducting.

Brandenburg concertos: The six Brandenburg concertos (BWV 1046-1051) by Johann Sebastian Bach are a collection of instrumental works presented to the Margrave of Brandenburg in 1721, but probably composed earlier.

P. 20

Incarcerated: Put or keep someone in prison or a place used as a prison.

P. 22

Milan period: A city of northern Italy, northeast of Genoa. Probably of Celtic origin, it was taken by the Romans in 222 BC and has been an important commercial, financial, cultural and industrial centre since medieval times because of its strategic location.

Mona Lisa: The Mona Lisa is a famous 16th-century portrait by Leonardo da Vinci.

Last Supper: Last Supper, in the New Testament is the meal taken by Jesus and his disciples on the eve of the passion. Jesus broke bread and passed a cup of wine among the disciples, identifying himself with the bread and the wine and linking the meal to his impending death on the cross. The meal was an anticipation, both of Jesus' death and of the eschatological banquet referred to in several Old Testament passages and by Jesus himself.

P. 24

Protestant: A Christian belonging to one of the three great divisions of Christianity (the other two are the Roman Catholic church and the Eastern Orthodox church). Protestantism began during the Renaissance as a protest against the established (Roman Catholic) church. That protest, led by Martin Luther, was called the Reformation, because it sprang from a desire to reform the church and cleanse it of corruption, such as the selling of indulgences. Protestants hold a great variety of beliefs, but they are united in rejecting the authority of the Pope.

P. 25

Guernica: Guernica is a historic town in the Basque region. It has metallurgical, furniture and food manufacturers, and some tourism. In April, 1937, German planes, aiding the insurgents in the Spanish civil war, bombed and destroyed Guernica. The indiscriminate killing of women and children aroused world opinion and the bombing of Guernica became a symbol of fascist brutality. The event inspired one of Picasso's most celebrated paintings. Guernica is also called *Guernica y Luno*.

Neo-classicism: A revival of classical aesthetics and forms, especially a revival in literature in the late 17th and 18th centuries, characterised by a regard for the classical ideals of reason, form and restraint. A revival in the 18th and 19th centuries in architecture and art, especially in the decorative arts, characterised by order, symmetry and simplicity of style. A movement in music lasting roughly from 1915 to 1940 that sought to avoid subjective emotionalism and to return to the style of the pre-Romantic composers.

P. 28

Surrealist movement: It is an artistic movement and an aesthetic philosophy that aims at the liberation of the mind by emphasising the critical and imaginative powers of the unconscious. Surrealism originated in early 20th century. European avant-garde art and literary circles, and many early surrealists were associated with the earlier Dad movement. Surrealism was an expressly revolutionary movement, encompassing actions intended to advance radical, political, social, cultural and personal change.

P. 29
Sheriff: Sheriff is both a political and a legal office held under the English common law or the person who holds such office.

P. 31
War of the Roses: Any of a series of intermittent civil wars in the 15th century between the English royal houses of York and Lancaster and their supporters. The wars began in the 1450s and ended in victory for the Lancastrians in 1485 with the death of Richard III at the Battle of Bosworth Field and the accession of Henry VII to the throne.

P. 32
Shahjahanabad: A city of north-central India on the Yamuna river. Important since ancient times, the old city was rebuilt by Shah Jahan in the 17th century with high stone walls enclosing the Red Fort that contained the imperial Mughal palace. The new part of Delhi became the capital of British India in 1912 and of independent India in 1947.
Taj Mahal: Taj Mahal is a mausoleum in Agra, Uttar Pradesh state, on the Yamuna river. It is considered one of the most beautiful buildings in the world and the finest example of the late style of Indian Islamic architecture. Mughal Emperor, Shah Jahan, ordered to build it after the death (1629) of his favourite wife, Mumtaz Mahal. The building, which was completed between 1632 and 1638, was designed by the local Muslim architect Ustad Ahmad Lahori. Set in its carefully laid out grounds, it is a reflection of the gardens of paradise to which the faithful ascend. The entire complex, with gardens, gateway structures and mosque was completed in 1643.
Pearl Mosque: The 'Pearl Mosque' is the name given to certain structures in more than one country. There is one in Lahore (Pakistan, built in 1991), second in Delhi inside Red Fort (built in 1569) and another is in Agra (built in 1647-53).

P. 33
CD-Rom: (Compact Disc Read Only Memory) A compact disc format used to hold text, graphics and hi-fidelity stereo sound.

P. 34
Holy Trinity: The Trinity is a river in north Texas flowing for 510 miles (820 km) south-east to Trinity Bay. The waters of upper tributaries and the main stream are impounded in numerous reservoirs that provide water for the Dallas-Fort Worth metropolitan area, for flood control, and for irrigation. The Trinity valley has a greater population and the majority of industrial development as opposed to other river basins in Texas. Massive flooding of the river occurred in the spring of 1990, recorded as among the nation's worst floods in the 20th century.

P. 36
Pseudonym: A name used instead of his or her real or original name by writers and actors.

P. 38
Fatehpur Sikri: A historic city of Uttar Pradesh, in north India. It was founded in 1569 by the Mughal Emperor Akbar to honour the Muslim saint, Sheikh Salim Chisti, who had foretold the birth of Akbar's son and heir, Jahangir.
Dyslexia: A disease in which one is unable to read and write. It is caused by the brain's inability to see the difference between some letter shapes.

P. 39
Kuomintang: Kuomintang is a political party of China. Sung Chiao-jen organised the party in 1912, under the nominal leadership of Sun Yat-sen, to succeed the Revolutionary Alliance. The original Kuomintang programme called for parliamentary democracy and moderate socialism.
Parkinson's disease: Parkinson's disease is a degenerative brain disorder first described by the English surgeon, James Parkinson in 1817. When there is no known cause, the disease usually appears after the age of 40 and is referred to as Parkinson's disease.

P. 40
Wheaties box: In 1934, the breakfast cereal, Wheaties, began the practice of including pictures of athletes on its packaging to coincide with its slogan 'The Breakfast of Champions'. In its original form, athletes were depicted on the sides or back of the cereal box, though in 1958, Wheaties began placing the pictures on the front of the box. The tradition has included hundreds of athletes from different sports and also team depictions.

P. 41
Arya Samaj: Arya Samaj is a Hindu reform movement in India that was founded by Swami Dayanand in 1875. He was a *sannyasin* (renouncer) who believed in the infallible authority of the *Vedas*. Dayanand advocated the doctrine of *karma* and reincarnation, and emphasised the ideals of *brahmacharya* (chastity) and *sanyasa* (renunciation).
Jallianwala Bagh: This garden derives its name from the owners of that piece of land known as village 'Jalla'. Jallianwala Bagh massacre involved the killing of hundreds of unarmed, defenceless Indians by a senior British military officer and took place on April 13, 1919 in the heart of Amritsar, the holiest city of Sikhs.

P. 44
Ramayana: Ramayana is one of the great Indian epics that tells about life in India around 1000 BC and offers models in *dharma*.
Mahabharata: A Sanskrit epic principally concerning the dynastic struggle and civil war between the Pandavas and the Kauravas in the kingdom of Kurukshetra around 9th century BC. It contains text of the *Bhagwad Gita*, numerous sub-plots and interpolations on theology, morals and statecraft.
Vedanta: The system of philosophy that further develops the implications in the *Upanishads* that all reality is a single principle, Brahman, and teaches that the believer's goal is to transcend the limitations of self-identity and realise one's unity with Brahman.

P. 45
Bolshevik revolution: The October Revolution, also known as the Bolshevik Revolution, was the second phase of the Russian revolution led by Bolsheviks under the leadership of Vladimir Lenin and marked the first officially communist revolution of the 20th

century, based upon the ideas of Karl Marx. The crucial revolutionary activities in Petrograd were under the command of the Petrograd Soviet's Military Revolutionary Committee.

P. 46
Mentally bifocal: Having two-foci thought.

P. 47
Tripos: Any of the examinations for the B.A. degree with honours at Cambridge University in England.

P. 49
Ecole Normale Superieure: This is an elite French *grande ecole*. Originally meant to train high school teachers through aggregation, it is now an elite institution training researchers, university professors and civil servants.
Crystallography: Crystallography (from the Greek words *crystallon* for 'solid' and *graphein* for 'write') is the experimental science of determining the arrangement of atoms in solids. In older usage, it was the scientific study of crystals.
Rabies: Rabies is a serious illness caused by a virus that infects the nervous system. Rabies produces a characteristic rapidly progressive disease of the central nervous system (brain and spinal chord nerves). Rabies is generally fatal if left untreated.

P. 50
Brahmo Samaj: Brahmo Samaj is a movement started by leading intellectuals of Bengal such as Raja Ram Mohan Roy in 1820s and which culminated in the birth of the Brahmo religion in 1850. Roy, through his organisation Brahmo Samaj, was among the first who fought to eliminate the practice of *sati*.
Vishwa Bharati: Vishwa Bharati is ensconced in a rural setting in the district of Birbhum, about 160 km from Kolkata. Academic session of the university is from 1 July to 30 June of next year and teaching begins as soon as the admission is over. The language courses usually begin in September.

P. 52
Ecole Militaire: The Royal Military Academy was founded by Louis XV in 1751, with the objective of making poor gentlemen into military men. Napoleon Bonaparte was trained here in 1784. The architect of the building, constructed in 1752, is Gabriel. The chapel where Napoleon graduated was not completed until 1769.
Battle of Waterloo: A battle in Belgium in 1815 in which the British and Prussians defeated the French under Napoleon Bonaparte. Napoleon abdicated as Emperor a few days after this final defeat, and a few weeks later he was captured and sent into exile.

P. 61
Bodyline: Bodyline was a cricketing tactic devised by the English cricket team for their 1932-33 tour of Australia, specifically to combat the extraordinary batting skill of Australia's Don Bradman. Bodyline bowlers deliberately aimed the cricket ball at the bodies of batsmen. This caused several injuries to Australian players and led to ill-feeling between the countries that rose to diplomatic levels.

P. 62
Shantiniketan: Tagore's university township is an itinerary that plots Bengal as a stopover, situated northwest of Kolkata. This is the place where Rabindranath Tagore lived and established this university.

P. 63
Grand Slam: This stands for major tournaments held in world tennis for individual players, both men and women and the palyers are ranked according to the tournaments they win. The Grand Slam title includes tennis championships of Britain (Wimbeldon), the USA, Australia and France.

P. 69
Purism: Strict observance of or insistence on traditional correctness, especially of language.

P. 72
Kung-fu: Kung fu is a well-known Chinese term used in the West to designate Chinese martial arts. Its original meaning is somewhat different, referring to one's expertise in any skill, not necessarily martial.

P. 73
Socrates: Socrates was a Greek philosopher, credited with laying the foundation for Western philosophical thought. His *Socratic Method* involved asking probing questions in a give and take which would eventually lead to the truth. Socrates's iconoclastic attitude did not sit well with everyone and at age 70 he was charged with heresy and corruption of local youth. Convicted, he carried out the death sentence by drinking hemlock and becoming one of history's earliest martyrs of conscience.

P. 75
Oscar: The Academy awards, commonly known as the Oscars, are the most prominent film awards in the world. The awards are granted by the Academy of Motion Picture Arts and Sciences, a professional honorary organisation which as of 2003 had a voting membership of 5,816 actors (with a membership of 1,311) making up the largest voting bloc.

P. 78
Jew: A member of the Hebrew people whose religion is Judaism.

P. 80
Madrasa: The word *madrasa* in the Arabic language and Persian, Turkish, Indonesian, etc. means a school for Muslims for the purpose of teaching children about religion.

P. 84
Malgudi: Malgudi is the fictitious town created by R.K.Narayan in his novel *Swami and Friends*. Narayan portrays Malgudi as a microcosm of India.

P. 85
Apartheid: System of racial segregation peculiar to the Republic of South Africa, the legal basis of which was largely repealed in 1991-92.

P. 86

Animated cartoons: A motion picture or television film consisting of a photographed series of drawings, objects, or computer graphics that simulates motion by recording very slight, continuous changes in the images, frame by frame.

P. 90

Shuttle mission: The shuttle is officially referred to in NASA jargon as the Space Transportation System (STS). Specific shuttle missions are therefore designated with the prefix STS.

P. 96

Nirmal Hriday: The name of this organisation translates into 'pure heart'. As a part of Mother Teresa's Missionaries of Charity, it serves as the home for the dying and the destitutes. It aims to fight poverty in Kolkata and provides beggars with food and medical facilities.